'If I did come 〔…〕 **want to earn n**〔…〕 **stipulated.**

He looked down his nose at her. 'The wife of a count does not work.'

'Then I couldn't stay here,' she whispered.

'Not for our son? Then do it for the life of luxury,' he said coldly. 'You will have a generous allowance and a credit card, the bills for which I will pay. On the condition that—'

'I'd be mad to agree! You would have a terrible hold over me,' she muttered. 'You could manipulate everything I did—'

'Forget what's gone on between us. Think of our son. All I want is for him to feel secure and happy.' He pushed his hands into his trouser pockets, looking worried. 'Surely you want that too? You see, Miranda, I will never let him go. He belongs here. This is his heritage, his right. Would you deny him that?'

'He needs to be loved more than he needs material wealth—' she began shakily.

'He will be loved!' Dante snapped.

Childhood in Portsmouth meant grubby knees, flying pigtails and happiness for **Sara Wood**. Poverty drove her from typist and seaside landlady to teacher, till writing finally gave her the freedom her Romany blood craved. Happily married, she has two handsome sons: Richard is married, calm, dependable, drives tankers; Simon is a roamer—silversmith, roofer, welder, always with beautiful girls. Sara lives in the Cornish countryside. Her glamorous writing life alternates with her passion for gardening, which allows her to be carefree and grubby again!

THE ITALIAN COUNT'S COMMAND

BY
SARA WOOD

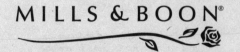

MILLS & BOON®

All the characters in this book have no existence outside the imagination of the author, and have no relation whatsoever to anyone bearing the same name or names. They are not even distantly inspired by any individual known or unknown to the author, and all the incidents are pure invention.

First published in Great Britain 2004
Harlequin Mills & Boon Limited,
Eton House, 18-24 Paradise Road, Richmond, Surrey TW9 1SR

© Sara Wood 2004

ISBN 0 263 83797 1

Set in Times Roman 10 on 11pt.
01-1204-55155

Printed and bound in Spain
by Litografía Rosés, S.A., Barcelona

CHAPTER ONE

'BAD news. You'd better brace yourself.' Unusually, his brother sounded sympathetic, his tone low and concerned.

Dante's fingers closed more tightly on his mobile phone. 'For what?' he shot, his heart going crazy in case his worst fears were realised.

'I'm sorry, Dante. I'm afraid that I have proof your wife is playing around.' Guido paused but Dante was too shocked to speak. 'I'm at your house now. She's upstairs. Drunk, out cold—and…well, I have to tell you that she's not wearing anything. There's concrete evidence that she's been entertaining a lover…'

His brother murmured on but Dante heard nothing. He had retreated into a world of stunned horror that slowly and surely turned to a white-hot fury till his Italian blood was boiling with volcanic rage.

It was true, then. All this time he'd been defending his wife of four years to his brother, insisting that she hadn't married his bank balance and that she *did* love him despite her cool reserve. It seemed he'd been wrong. Blinded by her beauty and her modesty.

Modesty? He gave a cynical laugh. Maybe even that had been assumed. Miranda's reserve had disappeared in a spectacular way whenever they'd made love. Fire hit his belly as he grimly acknowledged that he'd never known such pleasure. She was sensational in bed.

He drew in a sharp breath, pain searing through him as he reflected that maybe she'd had a lot of practice in the art of pleasing a man.

'Where's Carlo?' he jerked, praying that his son was safely with the nanny in some English park.

'Here in the house,' Guido said, to Dante's horror. 'Yelling his head off. I can't calm him.'

A burning sickness lurched in his stomach and he swore volubly in gutter Italian. Impotent rage began to cloud his judgement and wild, half-formed plans of revenge played havoc with his normally clear and balanced mind. Appalled by what was happening to him, he shook himself free of the red mist that demanded revenge for his wounded manhood and tried to hang on to his sanity.

He could hardly breathe but he managed to growl out, 'I'm in a taxi not far from my house. I'll be home in ten minutes or less.'

'Ten…! *What?!*' gasped Guido. 'B-but…you can't be! You're not supposed to be due back at Gatwick for two hours!'

'I caught an early flight… *Santo cielo!* What the hell does it matter?' he roared, losing his cool.

Guido seemed to be panicking about something but Dante had enough to worry about. Overwhelmed by helpless fury, he turned off his mobile and told the cabbie to drive like hell.

She was rocking. Being shaken. It hurt her head to move and she tried to ward her attacker off but her arms wouldn't do as they were told.

She groaned. Someone had put her entire skull in a pot and brought it to the boil. It was swelling inside, driving her mad. But at least the awful screaming had stopped at last. It had sounded like a child…

'Miranda! *Miranda!*'

Rough fingers gripped her arm as the grating tones pierced the chaos of her brain. She must be sick. That was it. Flu.

'Helllp mmme,' she mumbled through a thick and lolling tongue.

And found herself being lifted. Frightened, she found she could do nothing because her limbs had become paralysed. With a horrible swoop she was lowered onto the cold, hard tiles of what must be the shower.

'Open your eyes!' snarled a furious voice.

She couldn't. They'd been superglued. Oh, God! What was happening to her? She felt her stomach heave. And was suddenly sick.

Words whirled around her. Bitter, vicious words that she didn't understand. Her brain just wouldn't process them.

'Aaah!'

She choked and spluttered as a fierce spray of ice-cold water jetted straight into her face. It continued mercilessly, punishing her slumped body until she finally managed to open her eyes a fraction.

'Dante!' Seeing him, she felt a rush of sheer relief and gave a little sob. Everything would be all right now. His face hovered above hers, her fever making his features look threatening and distorted. Frightened, she clutched at the rim of the shower. 'Ill,' she muttered weakly.

'I wish. *You're drunk, you whore!*' he flung in disgust. And walked out.

Struck dumb by his reaction, she stayed crouched in the shower, incapable of making sense of this nightmare. That was it. A dream. She had a fever and this was an hallucination. If she closed her eyes she might wake up feeling better...

His mouth tightened as he strode off to check out the master bedroom thoroughly. Tangled sheets. Two bottles of champagne, two glasses. Miranda's clothes scattered haphazardly about the room. He swallowed. On the floor was a pair of men's briefs. And they weren't his.

There was the final proof. He felt his hand shaking as he accepted a glass of brandy from Guido.

'I did try to warn you a long while ago,' his brother said gently.

'I know.'

His own voice startled him. It had been nothing more than a whisper. The shock of Miranda's infidelity had taken away all his strength, all his pride and confidence. Rammed them both down his throat. Sat there laughing at him for being such a fool.

Knocking back the brandy, he returned to his son, who had been yelling his head off when he'd arrived. He'd gone to him first, of course. It had taken him several minutes to calm Carlo down. Finally his son had fallen asleep, utterly exhausted. Not until then had he gone to see what state Miranda was in because she wasn't important any more. She meant nothing.

He felt murderous that she'd abandoned their child while she partied in the next bedroom with her lover. That, he resolved, would never happen again.

Grimly he packed. Dazed, he accepted Guido's offer to keep an eye on his wife till she recovered. Full of pain, he caught up his sleeping son in his arms. And got the hell out of Miranda's life forever.

CHAPTER TWO

'THAT'S *it*!' Miranda announced tightly.

She was trying not to hyperventilate. Despite her shaking fingers, she managed to push the key in the lock of the Knightsbridge house and disable the alarm.

Her rasping breath tore at her lungs and she wondered how long she could hang on to the threads of apparent normality. It seemed her brain was stuck, the same thing going over and over in her mind till she wanted to scream in despair and hopelessness.

Despite all her efforts over the past two weeks she'd failed to trace her son—or her rat of a husband who'd abducted him. Her impulse was to kick something. Howl her eyes out in a darkened room. But she had something vital to do first.

Hauling her case indoors with a violence that betrayed her fractured nerves, she dropped the flight bag from her slim shoulder and strode through the hall to the phone. Her legs felt as if they belonged to someone else. She was amazed they obeyed her at all.

'No more faffing about. I'm going to call the police!' she muttered to her sister and snatched up the receiver, her finger poised to stab at the dial.

'*No!*' Lizzie looked appalled, then registered Miranda's astonished glance and gabbled on incoherently. 'I mean… well, we don't want to go public, do we? Think of the damage we'll do if we accuse Dante of *abduction*! The Severinis *exist* on their good name…'

Lizzie rambled on, mystifyingly defending the indefensible. Miranda fumed. 'What do I care?' she snapped.

She couldn't believe her sister's reluctance to bring the whole Severini family to book. Not one of them had an honourable bone in the whole of their aristocratic, self-serving body.

A silent rage boiled within her as her husband's handsome, savagely cruel face swam before her eyes. Almost immediately she felt a lurch of misery and realised with helpless despair that this entirely new image of him was causing her untold grief.

Bleakly she stared at the purring phone. She wanted the old Dante Severini back. The adoring, sensual man who'd wooed and married her within a month. Not that calculating monster who'd treated her so callously and had taken her child away. She choked back a sob and realised she was too upset to speak.

Shaking, she replaced the phone in its cradle, intent on keeping up an appearance of self-control. If she let out her true feelings, she knew that she'd probably smash the entire contents of the house in frustration before sinking into a morass of self-pity.

It was sheer will-power alone that held her slender body rigid and erect. She was unbelievably tired but she couldn't let up, wouldn't give in to what she saw as weakness. Never had, never would, whatever the challenge.

'I must call in the authorities. We've spent the past fourteen days jetting around, trying to trace Dante's whereabouts,' she said coldly. 'And,' she added, 'I've had my fill of those Severini lackeys who clam up the moment his name is mentioned.'

'It's company policy—' Lizzie began.

'I said I was his wife!' she snapped. 'Showed them my passport!'

'They'd had instructions from Dante about an impostor—'

'How *dare* he do that to me?' Miranda fumed. 'I've never been so humiliated in all my life! Being escorted off the premises by security men…!'

Thinking of the terrible wall of silence she'd encountered from Dante's continental staff in some of the major capitals of Europe, she jerked up her head stubbornly. This was *war*.

'I want my son,' she clipped in a curt understatement.

'And…' Her voice faltered before she could rally it. She swallowed. 'He'll be wanting me.'

In a quick movement she turned away, ostensibly to make the call, but it was a means of hiding the sudden rush of tears that blurred the steely blue of her agonised gaze.

The word 'want' didn't begin to describe her need—or Carlo's. It was more visceral than just missing him desperately. It was as if part of her had been ripped away to leave a raw and bleeding wound.

But Carlo would be suffering more deeply. He wouldn't understand why she wasn't there any more, why she didn't tuck him up in bed, cuddle him and play with him…

'Oh, dear heaven!' she whispered under her breath.

Thinking about him, and how miserable he must be, she felt as if swords were being plunged into her body over and over again.

But tears weren't an option. She needed to stay calm and alert. On no account could she afford to surrender to the misery and fear that churned in her stomach, which kept her awake long into the bleak and empty night.

A small, stifled moan escaped her pale lips. No child! No husband! And she'd loved them both with such an all-consuming passion…

At that moment the phone rang, its shrillness startling her so profoundly that she grabbed it and clamped it to her ear, her nerves scattered into pitiful shreds as she answered without thinking, almost spitting out her name.

'Yes? Miranda here!'

There was a crackling sound and then silence, giving her the opportunity to regain her composure. So she took a deep breath and began again.

'Miranda Severini. Who's there?' she asked, sounding several degrees cooler in tone.

'Dante.'

Dante! The shock at hearing the caressing murmur was so great that she staggered. In desperation her elegant hand caught at the marble-topped table, the force of the movement breaking a nail. Blindly she stared at its jagged edge, her mind racing.

Contact with him at last! Suddenly her heart thundered with hope but she didn't give her husband the satisfaction of hearing her plead for her own child. She knew she'd either scream at him hysterically or be choked into silence by her tears.

Pride prevented her from offering him either of those alternatives. With a supreme effort she schooled herself to remain silent, waiting for him to continue while her heart thudded and jerked painfully within her chest.

'Miranda? *Dica!* Speak!'

Annoyingly the huskily spoken words seeped into her very veins. He'd always split her name into three lyrical syllables; Mee-rahn-dah. And to her dismay, memories of their love-filled days briefly melted the marrow of her very bones.

Then she clenched her teeth to remind herself of Guido's revelation. On that fateful day when she'd had that terrible fever, her brother-in-law had poured coffee into her and brought blankets so that she could curl up on the sofa.

She'd known that Dante had gone off with Carlo, but didn't understand why. Everything had been such a blur. Guido's sympathy with her plight had caused him to spill the beans.

He'd told her that Dante had married her for the sake of his inheritance. Apparently he had fathered her son purely to curry favour with his childless uncle. The moment Dante's uncle had died and the inheritance was safely in the bag, he'd spirited Carlo away, too cowardly to face her out.

She frowned, pieces of the jigsaw of that day still missing. It puzzled her that her bed had been in such a mess, though she supposed she must have tossed and turned in her fevered state. But she couldn't understand what the empty champagne bottles were doing in the rubbish bin, or why two glasses were in the wrong cupboard.

'Miranda!'

'Yes? You have something to say to me?' she prompted, as if Dante were a casual friend who should be apologising for a rude remark, and not the man who'd scattered her trust and love to the four winds.

Love! Her lip quivered. He had become her enemy. A heartless brute who'd told her in an e-mail that she'd seen the last of him and Carlo. *And* that she wouldn't get a penny from him—but could support herself by whoring! Whatever had brought that on? He'd also accused her of being drunk. Was he trying to make out a case for divorce?

There was a silence. She could hear his regular breathing. He was deliberately toying with her. He must know how frantic she'd be!

Gritting her teeth, she fought to hold back her fury. In the huge, ornate mirror she unexpectedly caught sight of herself. She stared at the woman who bore no resemblance to how she felt inside.

To all appearances she was an ice-cool ash-blonde, immaculately groomed despite just returning from the tedious trawl to Dante's offices in France, Spain and Milan, the chignon still smooth, the understated cream suit the epitome of classy designer elegance.

Except that she could see—despite the impeccable make-up—there were tell-tale signs of bruised, tired eyes beneath, and that her pale gold skin no longer glowed or reflected the light but seemed as dead as she felt, deep in her heart.

All her inner turmoil, she vowed, would be kept from Dante. He'd never know how badly he'd hurt her. Play the victim, she'd decided, and she'd become the victim.

Besides, Carlo needed her to be strong. Tough. On the ball. For you, my darling son, she thought, I'd bite my tongue till it bleeds.

'Dante,' she said, injecting a faint element of boredom into her voice, 'I have a call to make. Get on with it.'

His breath hissed in with sharp displeasure. She'd chosen the blunt words deliberately. Dante loathed ugly speech.

'I do apologise if I am ringing you at an inconvenient time,' he drawled, heavily lacing his words with sarcasm. 'I am aware that you don't give a damn about my son. I also know that looking after him interfered with your own selfish needs. However, I did think you might ask how he is, perhaps out of social politeness…'

She shut out his scathing tones as he continued to berate her in that vein. Of course her only thought was for her child! Her impulse was to yell at the top of her voice, to demand if Carlo was missing her. To plead to be told where Dante had taken their son…

But she held back. Dante would love her to beg and she wouldn't give him the satisfaction. Not in a million years.

She'd worked for him as his UK secretary before they'd married four years ago. Even then she'd known that beneath his smooth charm lay a shrewd obstinacy and ruthless drive that ensured he always achieved his goals.

Unbeknown to her, he'd needed a wife urgently to secure a fabulous inheritance—and she'd been there, sitting on a plate, ready to be gobbled up. She blushed to think of her joyous acceptance of his proposal.

With his uncle's recent death he had acquired the power to buy whatever he wanted—including, should there be a battle, the custody of their child. She trembled, scared of the might ranged against her.

From his penthouse in Milan, Dante's bachelor uncle had ruled the Severini silk empire. The family silk mills in northern Italy supplied the great fashion houses of the world. She'd never realised that Dante had been poised in the wings to take over the reins. He'd never told her. But then she'd never figured in his future plans, so why should he?

It was a nightmare situation. Her husband would want his son to inherit. That meant she'd effectively lost Carlo—unless she played her trump card: her threat to dishonour the Severinis.

On the flight back to England after her fruitless quest to discover Dante's whereabouts, she'd decided to publicly expose him for what he was: a ruthless, selfish manipulator who cared nothing for people's feelings. Whose naked ambition and obsessive pride had caused him to rip a three-year-old from his mother's loving care.

Oh, God! she thought with a lurch of sickening misery. Carlo would be so bewildered! How dared Dante use her as a brood mare and rip her son away?

Fiercely she tried to shut out the poignant vision of the dark-eyed angel who had illuminated her life. His sweet face with its ready smile had haunted her since his disappearance. It had been the hardest thing in the world not to break down and indulge in an orgy of weeping. And she was at the end of her tether now.

'Dante,' she interrupted wearily, breaking in on his vitriolic assassination of her character, 'is this why you've called? To vent your spleen? To kid yourself that I'm to blame for your actions? If so, I am hanging up now—'

'*No!*'

She felt a small stab of satisfaction at that hastily rapped 'no'. He needed something. Hopefully her—to take Carlo back. Maybe he'd decided he could return Carlo to her, and make babies—correction—descendants, with some other woman, now that he'd safely inherited his uncle's fortune.

She felt sick at that thought. A small part of her still loved Dante. Sighing, she acknowledged that you couldn't switch off a grand passion like a light.

But at least her gamble—of appearing to be indifferent to his cruelty—had paid off. He'd been thrown off balance. Her reaction to his call had not been what he'd expected. That was how you handled bullies. It disconcerted them.

Trying not to raise her hopes, she pressed a hand hard against her thudding heart, crushing the rich silk jacket beneath her long fingers. And, keeping her breathing as light as possible, she enquired merely,

'Well?'

'*Che Dio mi aiuti!* You are a cold, unfeeling monster of a woman!' he spat.

Miranda almost sobbed out loud. *He* had turned her into an

ice queen. It had been her only defence against his growing indifference over the past year.

She managed to hold herself together. 'I assume you'll get to the point eventually.'

Mentally urging him on with an almost hysterical panic, she sank to her knees, which seemed dangerously liquid. She saw Lizzie staring at her, a frozen expression on her face, and was touched that her sister felt so agitated on her behalf.

Dante cleared his throat. 'You must come to Italy. It is imperative that you do.' It sounded as if a herd of wild elephants were dragging the words from him. His normally satiny voice was harsh and begrudging. 'I've sent a ticket by courier. The flight is tomorrow. My chauffeur will meet you. I'm at my late uncle's estate.'

Oh, thank you, thank you! she cried in silent passion. He'd relented! No, she corrected. That seemed unlikely. He'd rather cut off his right hand.

More probably, she thought rapidly, he'd discovered that looking after Carlo in strange surroundings was harder than he'd imagined. Heavens, she thought with a rare flash of wasp-ishness, he must have been desperate to swallow his pride!

But Carlo would be hers. The separation was to end. Her hand flew to her mouth to stop herself from groaning with heartfelt relief. She'd have him back, safe in her arms. *Tomorrow!*

All of a sudden, she couldn't contain herself any longer. And without even responding to her husband's imperious demand, she put the phone down with a crash.

Then burst into floods of tears. And, embarrassed, she ran up to her room to give vent to her relief in private.

Lizzie gaped. She'd never seen her sister cry. Not even seven years ago, on the day their mother had died when she was twelve and Miranda eighteen. And since their father had left them all before their mother's death, Miranda had then become the breadwinner and substitute mother.

Dante had been the first person to get under Miranda's skin, the first man to make her blossom and go starry-eyed. But then he was gorgeous, even Lizzie had to admit, more charismatic than his handsome younger brother, Guido, who managed the London office.

Guiltily Lizzie chewed her lip. She dreaded what Miranda might say if she ever found out she was dating the wild and reckless Guido. But she had a life too, didn't she? The Severini family was rich and she wanted *in*. It was scary now that Miranda had been cast aside with no income and the prospect of homelessness.

With a shudder, Lizzie remembered the penny-pinching days of her childhood. Since Miranda's marriage, she'd become used to living in the lovely house here in Knightsbridge, and charging all her shopping to Dante's account.

So with Miranda possibly blowing the chance she'd had to be one of the idle rich, she, Lizzie, had to take over the running now. If Dante didn't take her sister back, Lizzie thought, she'd bag herself a Severini of her own to provide the luxury lifestyle she craved.

'Look at it! Miranda, just clock this place!' Lizzie screeched.

Miranda was beginning to regret agreeing to her sister's plea to be found a place on the flight too. For the whole journey, Lizzie had been pestering her to reconcile with Dante. In addition, Lizzie's envy of the sumptuous villa on the shores of Lake Como had made Miranda squirm.

Meeting the chauffeur's cynical gaze in the driving mirror, she looked away in embarrassment. Then she realised that the car had stopped in front of some imposing gates. She tensed. They must have reached their destination.

Her stomach began to churn like a washing machine and she forgot Lizzie's embarrassing worship of conspicuous wealth. In a few moments Carlo would be snuggling up to her. She could hardly breathe for excitement.

'Miranda, this is money with a capital M!' gloated Lizzie. 'Couldn't you try to patch things up? Oh, please, please! Look what you'd be missing—'

'I've told you!' Miranda frowned with impatience. 'I'm here

for one reason only and that's to take Carlo from that swine I stupidly married! I swear,' she cried with low and heartfelt passion, 'that I will move heaven and earth if necessary to take my baby back to England—'

'You're hopeless! All right. Get a damn good divorce settlement at the very least,' counselled Lizzie crossly. 'Screw him for all you can.'

The massive wrought-iron gates swung open electronically. As the limo purred through them, Miranda's face lit up with relief and she couldn't prevent a warm smile from seeping out at the thought of her son's dear little body, soon to be held close to hers.

With a start, she noticed that the chauffeur's eyes had hardened at the sight of her pleasure and she wondered what Dante had told his staff about her.

'Is this actually Dante Severini's house?' she asked, breathless with excitement.

There was a moment's hesitation before a grudging grunt. '*Si.*'

Not '*Si, signora,*' the usual courteous response, she noted. Miranda gritted her teeth at the deliberate insult and then dismissed it. What did it matter what lies Dante had told? She'd be shot of the lot of them in an hour and on her way back home.

The car crawled up the long driveway and her tension mounted. So this, she thought in amazement, was the estate that Dante had coveted, along with the business!

She could see why. It was breathtakingly situated on the shores of Lake Como in the north of Italy. The gardens had been laid out in a mixture of English and Italian styles, so that rhododendrons and azaleas and plane trees harmonised surprisingly well with the palms and banana plants set amid elegant terraces and statues.

And she'd never even known of its existence.

'Jumping elephants!' Lizzie shrieked as the house finally came into view. 'My brother-in-law's become a billionaire at least! Jammy devil!'

'Lizzie!' she scolded, humiliated by the chauffeur's disgusted glance.

'What? I'm only saying what's true,' protested her sister. 'Forget the divorce. You're looking great, Miranda. This is your big chance. Play your cards right as we discussed, get back into his bed, and life'll be a ball!'

Miranda was barely listening, far more interested in studying the house. Four storeys high, the pale ochre building was both graceful and imposing. An eighteenth-century palace, fit for a prince. Or a highly ambitious man.

It was quite the most beautiful house she had ever seen, straight out of a fairy tale. It sat serenely in the lush green gardens, with what must be magnificent views over the stunning blue lake.

Yet despite its grandeur the house seemed welcoming and friendly as if centuries of love and care had given it a mellow personality of its own.

Even Lizzie had been silenced as they came to a halt by the broad stone staircase.

Now I truly understand why he schemed with such desperation, Miranda mused soberly. This was a prize that Dante could not bear to lose. Even if it meant deliberately deceiving a woman he knew was madly in love with him. Why not marry the poor sap and give her a little happiness for a short time, before consigning her to the rubbish heap?

Miranda's heart beat a tattoo in her chest as she slid from the luxurious car. Trembling with anticipation and almost sick with excitement and joy, she watched Dante's tall figure emerge from the imposing house and concentrated on dealing with the way her heart contracted at the sight of him. Behind her, Lizzie tumbled out, still rhapsodising in ear-splitting shrieks to some boyfriend on her mobile.

A jolt of disappointment hit her. *Just* Dante had appeared. No Carlo. Her stomach lurched with fear and then she steadied herself. Carlo must be having a nap. She smiled, as lovingly remembered images of her sleeping son filled her mind.

And smiling adoringly still, she lifted her gaze to the man

who was watching her so intently. A spark of electricity leapt across the distance between them. The impact of seeing him was just the same as the first day she'd met him: a deep, visceral belonging, a sense of a shared destiny and warm, overwhelming joy.

Except, she sighed, those feelings had always been one-sided. He'd never loved her. And of course now she understood what lay behind his autocratic bearing and the air of perfect grooming, the perfectly tailored silk suit in a discreet honey colour, the made-to-measure casual cream shirt, and those expensive leather shoes.

Money. Buckets of it. And breeding.

She'd been ignorant of all this. When they'd lived in London their lifestyle had been comfortable but not excessively so. Now she knew that he and his family were in a different league altogether, that of the mega-rich.

She gulped, intimidated by this because he had become a stranger, just by stepping into the higher echelons of Italian society.

The chauffeur hurried up the steps to meet Dante and was gesticulating and talking rapidly. Probably, Miranda thought uncomfortably, complaining about Lizzie's high-decibel shrieks and embarrassing remarks. Dante's eyes narrowed in a suspicious stare and her composure wilted like her body in the blazing sun as she blushed with shame.

'You'd think Carlo would be waiting for you,' Lizzie complained. 'Unless Dante's teaching you a lesson and we've come on a wild-goose chase.'

Fear rooted Miranda to the ground. Had she been dragged here for revenge? To be given hope, only to be told that she could whistle for her son?

'He'll…be asleep,' she said, not very convincingly.

Carlo…*where? When?* she thought desperately, trying to contain herself. In panic, she listened for the sounds of a child but heard nothing, only a tension-filled silence.

Feeling chilled to the core despite the hot sun, she waited for Dante to come to her because she couldn't move an inch.

Eventually he dismissed the chauffeur and his long, impec-
cably clad legs slowly began to descend the steps.

With infuriating nonchalance, Dante paused on the bottom
step, reaching out casually to fiddle with a cascade of
geraniums in an antique copper urn.

Drat him, he must know what she was going through! She'd
wring his neck if he continued to play with her feelings!

'Miranda.' He gave her a mocking bow. No kiss. No hand-
shake. No touching. So she just nodded back, managing to
seem cool and contained. 'Greetings, Elizabeth,' he murmured
to his star-struck sister-in-law. 'Perhaps you would enjoy tour-
ing the house. Make yourself at home, and help yourself to
champagne and pastries in the salon.'

'Cool! You bet!' Eyes sparkling and with her mobile still
clamped to her ear, Lizzie leapt up the steps, blissfully unaware that Dante had skilfully got her out of the way.

His mocking dark eyes followed her sister and his lips
curved in a faintly contemptuous smile, the sensual, cresting
wave of his mouth sending shivers of remembrance down
Miranda's back.

She closed her eyes briefly as her body felt the cascade of
kisses he used to shower on her. All carefully calculated, she
thought bitterly, to keep her sweet until his uncle died! Cured
of her stupid mooning, she snapped open her eyes again.

With a total lack of urgency, Dante turned to Miranda. His
gaze slid up her taut body in an arrogant assessment of her
graceful figure in the classically cut silk dress and jacket. In
Dante's favourite cornflower-blue, it matched her eyes. Into
which, she'd thought with a pang of anguish when she'd selected it, he'd gazed with such devastating results.

'You are thinner,' he announced, his frown registering his
disapproval.

She bridled immediately. Once she'd loved his intrinsically
Italian interest in her body and clothes. Now his interest was
insulting and intrusive. She lifted her shoulders in an eloquent
uninterest.

'My appearance is none of your business. Naturally I've been busy. Rushing here, dashing there…'

And from feeling sick at the sight of food. With agonising cramps in her stomach. Damn you, Dante! she inwardly seethed. Where is my son?

He corrected the frown which had drawn his brows together.

'You're right. Your appalling lifestyle in England is no concern of mine any longer, I am glad to say. Tea has been brought to my study,' he said icily. 'Follow me.' When he began to climb the steps again she made no reply but stomped along behind him in silence, trying not to rise to his insult. 'Nothing to say to me?' he shot back at her.

'No.' She'd bide her time. See what he had to say—

'I thought as much,' he scorned as she caught him up. 'You've just proved something to me.'

'Oh? What might that be?'

'That when I was around you only pretended that you loved Carlo.'

'How on earth do you arrive at that conclusion?' she demanded indignantly.

'You've been separated from him for two weeks. But you haven't bothered to ask where he is,' he said with bitter contempt.

So much for his intuition, she thought, intensely irritated. Didn't he know her whole mind was screaming for information?

'I saw no point in wasting my breath. I imagined,' she retorted drily, proud that there was hardly a tremor in her voice at all, 'that you would tell me when you're good and ready and not before.'

He gave a grunt of acknowledgement. 'How well you know me, Miranda!' he muttered, indicating that they should enter the building.

Know him? On the contrary. How could you know a devious, deceitful snake? She would never trust him again. Suddenly, doubts as to his motive for bringing her here filled her head and she came to a halt.

'Just tell me one thing,' she said evenly, 'otherwise I see no reason to go any further. Am I going to see my son soon?'

'Oh, yes.' Dante's eyes flickered. 'I give you my guarantee that the two of you will be reunited. Please enter. We will talk inside.'

Her breath shuddered out. It seemed that her fears were groundless and all she needed to do was keep her dignity until Dante relented and let her take Carlo into her arms. Only then would she risk giving way to joy. And tears. She could hardly believe it. The nightmare was almost over.

CHAPTER THREE

SUDDENLY she felt unbelievably tired. It was as though all her mental and physical energies had carried her through to this moment. Now she and Carlo were about to be reunited, she could begin to let go.

Exhaustion washed over her as she followed his tall figure through the huge carved doors. If anything, he seemed better-looking than ever. Her resentful eyes noted the perfect curve that his neat black hair made on the rich, dark skin of his neck. The breadth of his shoulders in the crisp Milanese jacket.

And in her mind's eye she could see his sensational back as if he were naked: the firmness of its triangular shape, the slender hips and tight, neat buttocks. The smooth flesh golden and inviting her touch, muscles moving beneath the well-fitted clothes, the thick cords on either side of his spine proclaiming his athleticism and physical power.

Her heart ached. She could have wept for everything they had lost. Not only those sweet, amazingly fierce explosions of erotic pleasure they'd shared, but also the intimacy, the companionship of the early years together. Even, she sighed, if that had been not real, but a clever deception on his part so that she had suspected nothing while his uncle was alive.

It had been an arranged marriage. The trouble was, she hadn't known that. Her spirits sank lower.

'Welcome to my home.'

He turned to her as though he might be inviting her opinion of it. She made a show of looking around as if that was what she'd been doing all along.

The *palazzo*—for that was what it must surely be—seemed no longer friendly, but daunting in its grandeur. In the cool darkness of the shuttered hall, glass and gold gleamed mysteriously. As they crossed the marble floor, her stilettos tapped with an intrusive echo.

Dante's ancestors, captured in oils and enclosed in ornate gold frames, checked her out, their dark eyes following her speculatively as she and Dante approached the theatrical double staircase.

Her surroundings had the effect of making her feel uncomfortable. These were riches on a grand scale. Few ambitious men could have remained indifferent when tempted with such luxury, such power, and the prospect of heading a five-hundred-year-old dynasty.

If only she hadn't been caught in Dante's honey trap! Guido had explained that his brother knew she had fallen in love with him. Dante had leapt at the chance to marry hastily, before his sick uncle had carried out his threat to leave everything to a more distant, married member of the family.

She winced. The scheming Dante must have waited to hear of his uncle's death like a vulture hovering over a sick animal. No wonder he'd enquired after Amadeo Severini's health so often and so earnestly. Her eyes hardened. It must have been very frustrating when Amadeo had hung on to life for nearly four more years!

'What do you think of the house?' Dante asked coolly. 'Does it appeal to your tastes?'

Her frosty gaze slanted chillingly in his direction. 'I'm sure you don't care about my opinion.'

'It interests me to know what you think.'

Haughtily she lifted her chin. She had no intention of bolstering his inflated ego. 'Too big for one man,' she said in dismissal.

'I agree,' he said to her surprise, pausing as they reached the top of the stairs. 'That's why Amadeo didn't live here and just used it for entertaining.'

'But you will?' she hazarded, her eyes narrowing, knowing the answer. He clearly adored his new position. He'd sacrificed a good deal for it.

'Correct.'

The first doubt slid into her mind. If he thought it was too big for him on his own...surely he wasn't thinking of keeping Carlo! Her pulses began to quicken with alarm but she hid her apprehension. Whatever game he was playing, he'd see no sign of weakness from her. Perhaps, she consoled herself, he was planning for his mother to join him. And Guido.

'I was always under the impression that Amadeo's main residence was the penthouse in Milan,' she observed icily. 'You didn't tell me he owned a *palazzo* as well.'

And the implicit question was there: why not?

Dante regarded her with unreadable eyes. 'I had my reasons.'

'Which were?' she pushed.

He hesitated and then said in a flat tone, 'I had hoped that you would be marrying me for the person I was, not for any material benefits I could give you.'

So he'd wanted to be loved! Huh! She felt like hitting him. He'd wanted someone so wrapped up in him that he could remain in control. Someone who didn't matter to him. What about her? Hadn't she been entitled to love, too?

'You were wrong,' she snapped. Wrong to marry her for convenience. Wrong to use her.

'So I have discovered,' he growled.

Grim-faced, he set off again, striding so fast along the broad landing that she had to half-run to keep up.

'Talking about houses,' he flung back at her curtly, 'I might as well tell you that I am selling my place in Knightsbridge. I will live here in future.'

'Suits me,' she muttered.

Coming to a halt in front of an enormous pair of double doors flanked by huge Chinese vases, he glanced without pity at her glacial profile.

'I'm not sure you realise the implications. When the Knightsbridge house is sold, you will have nowhere to live,' he informed her, clearly imagining she would gasp with horror.

So she did nothing of the kind. She'd manage. Always had.

'I expected no less from you,' she assured him loftily and was pleased when he flushed at the insult.

Despite Lizzie's urging to take Dante to the cleaners, she'd decided to keep her dignity and independence. Apart from a modest maintenance for Carlo, she wouldn't take a penny from him. She'd rather starve than be beholden to a man who'd treated her so callously.

Dante scowled at her. 'My lawyers will see that you get nothing from me in a divorce settlement. You can support yourself.'

'Yes. There's always whoring,' she said sarcastically, reminding him of his vile suggestion on the e-mail. She felt some satisfaction when he stiffened, his entire body taut with suppressed fury. Glancing at the door and with her stomach doing somersaults, she asked, 'Is Carlo in here?'

'No,' he snapped. 'It's my study. Come in.'

Her disappointment was profound. Apparently she was to wait till Carlo woke up. And she could do nothing to hurry him. Out of sheer spite, he'd make her wait. Well, wait she would. As long as it took.

Dante opened the door and with a characteristic, gentlemanly gesture he stood to one side. But his manners were only superficial. No gentleman would have behaved so badly.

Steeling herself to perhaps an hour of hanging around, Miranda stalked into the room—only to catch her breath in wonder.

'Oh! That's incredible!' she whispered in reluctant awe.

Her huge eyes were fixed on the open glass doors on the opposite side of the room, which framed the most wonderful view she'd ever seen in the whole of her life. Drawn to it, unable to resist its invitation, she crossed the Persian-carpeted floor and stepped onto the balcony outside as if in a dream. But when she placed her hands on the wrought-iron rail, she found it was hot to her hands and snatched them away with a small cry.

'I should have warned you,' Dante muttered.

Striding rapidly out to join her, he turned her hands over

and examined her palms, frowning at the pale pink bar of heat on each one. For a moment she felt dizzy, assailed equally by heavenly perfumes from the garden and the nearness of him—his flawless olive skin, the dark brows and thick black lashes, that peaking mouth she had kissed and tasted and hungered for so many times.

'It's…nothing!' she insisted huskily. 'I'm fine!' Shaken by her lingering desires, she stared up at him in dismay.

And, looking a little startled by her halting protest, he jerked his hands from hers, which were tingling, darn them, and that was nothing to do with the very minor marks on her palms. Because she also tingled down the entire length of her body and way, way within. Delicious. Devastating. She shifted unhappily.

'Not hurt at all, then,' he drawled.

'It would take more than that to wound me,' she retorted, hating his sarcastic tone.

'Yes. You have a monumentally thick skin.'

'I'd call it a determination to tough things out,' she countered.

And, taking a deep breath, she concentrated on the reason she'd come out to the balcony: to drink in the magical view and to take a minute or two to recover her energies before she could collect Carlo and start the journey home.

As she thought of that wonderful moment, almost immediately her shoulders relaxed. And because there was nothing else to do till her son woke from his sleep, she surrendered to the enjoyment of the scene before her. Even the most uptight person would have been entranced and she was momentarily spellbound, gazing at the view in rapt silence.

'What do you think of Lake Como?' Dante asked, close by and strangely tense.

'I've never seen anything like this. It's stunning,' she replied softly.

'Quite breathtaking,' he growled.

'It must be a glorious view to see when you wake. How long have you been here?' she enquired curiously.

Only inches away from her, he replied, 'A week.' When she nodded and continued to gaze dreamily ahead, he muttered under his breath something that sounded like, *'Irresistibile.'*

Her head jerked around, her eyes wide and startled. 'What?'

He frowned. 'The view.' His eyes became cruelly mocking. 'Surely you didn't think I meant you?'

'Hardly!' Hastily she dragged her brain into gear. She would keep calm. She must maintain her dignity.

'To me,' he said, 'this place is more beautiful, more precious, than all the paintings on the walls, all the priceless antiques in the house. It is simply the perfection of nature.'

She wondered why he was giving the house the hard sell. To make her envious? Or... She swallowed nervously. To force her to agree that Carlo would be better off here?

Dante certainly seemed besotted with his inheritance. Though it wasn't surprising. Like him, she gazed with appreciation across the lake at the huddle of ochre and sienna houses of the little villages nestling at the foot of wooded hills. High mountains—she presumed the Alps—rose behind them, their peaks slicing jaggedly into the sky.

Wildness and serenity combined. An extraordinary combination and one that reached deep into her and touched her heart.

Beside her, Dante shifted imperceptibly. She could feel his very warmth and detected the faint hint of vanilla, which perfumed his favoured aftershave and shower lotion. That—or tiredness—made her quiver.

'You must be thrilled with what's landed in your lap,' she remarked with deliberate tartness, fighting her attraction for him.

He studied her, his gaze lingering a little too long for her comfort. 'I am,' he admitted. 'Smell that air.'

'Yes.' She leaned cautiously over the balcony. 'What is that wonderful scent?'

'It comes from the fragrant ozmanthus by the pergola.'

'It's very intense,' she said jerkily, bemused by the electric atmosphere. And all she could do was to utter banalities in the hope that her pulse rate would consequently fall.

Dante muttered something under his breath. 'Yes. It's the heat. And because there's not a breath of wind. Como has many moods, which can change by the hour. At the moment the water could almost be a sheet of glass,' he mused idly into the hushed, heady air, saturated with the divine scent.

Miranda despaired. Despite her suspicions about his motives for enthusing about the house, she was holding her breath again, unable to take her eyes from his rapturous face, which the late-afternoon sun had lit so that his profile looked as if it had been carved from beaten gold.

With a jolt she realised an unpalatable fact. He loved this house more than he'd ever loved her.

Tartly she hoped he'd be very happy with it. And that it would keep him satisfied at night. His love affair with the house was all-embracing. Well, she'd rather have the love of her child. She fidgeted, anxious now to turn the conversation to Carlo, but he spoke before she could do so.

'There was a violent storm that night we first came,' he reminisced in a low murmur, seemingly in no hurry to see if her son was awake. Impatiently she listened, watching his expressive face, loving, hating, and hurting. 'I discovered that the lake can be dangerous. Like a tempestuous woman.' His dark eyes seemed to simmer like hot coals as they settled on hers. 'The water was not the deceptively calm surface we see now. It was wild and turbulent. And exciting at the same time.'

Something jerked inside her. What was he doing? The curl of his sensual mouth left her in no doubt as to his meaning. He'd often commented on the passion that simmered beneath her own cool exterior. Miranda struggled for mastery over the sudden rush of sexual hunger he'd deliberately aroused.

It was hardly surprising she still felt stirrings of desire. They'd been so good together. Shockingly uninhibited. They'd made love everywhere, any time, seemingly unable to get enough of one another.

Guido had put her straight about that. 'Every man will grab

the chance of having sex,' he'd explained. 'Doesn't matter what the woman's like. And Dante's the most over-sexed man I know.'

She bit her lip. Had it just been sex and nothing else? Had he needed the strong stimulation of those erotic situations so that he could make love to her? She shrank from that explanation. It would be too humiliating.

Maybe everyone behaved as they did in private. She wouldn't know. She was still naive, an innocent, with no other lover for comparison. At twenty-one, when they'd become lovers, she'd been untutored in the more intimate side of a relationship. He had awoken her to unbelievable delights and had cracked her ice-maiden image where sex was concerned.

Their first carnal encounter had been incredible and he'd reached a hitherto unknown, passionate side of her that had amazed them both. Over time their lovemaking had become even better, blissful and fulfilling. *For her.* She winced.

Every inch still burned for him, ached for the wonderful release that sex gave to her body. She groaned inwardly. It had been a mistake to let her mind run on like this!

Appalled, she averted her face to hide the flush of heat that tormented her from deep inside, through her protesting flesh and pulsing veins and out to her scorched skin.

'Few things are what they seem on the surface,' she muttered, thinking of his urbane manner and inner cruelty. 'Maggots seem to head for the best-looking apple. It's only when you bite into it that you discover the rotten core. Nothing's perfect, is it?'

He scowled. 'True. Though this view comes close to perfection. Perhaps that's why I cannot resist it,' he said cynically. 'It will never be sullied.'

He drew in a huge breath, as if regretting that the same couldn't be said for his wife. Miranda opened her mouth to demand to see Carlo but infuriatingly he forestalled her again.

'My ancestors chose well to build the *palazzo* here three hundred years ago. My friends are envious.' He hesitated and said carefully, 'They all agree that anyone would leap at the chance to live here.'

Miranda's eyes narrowed. He was excusing himself for succumbing to devious means to get his hands on the house.

'It is very beautiful,' she agreed coolly and drew breath to ask about Carlo.

'The Severinis have always had an eye for beauty.'

Despite her anxiety, his velvety murmur fed her libido unnervingly. She sensed he was gazing at her and not the view, but this time she didn't turn to confirm this. Didn't dare. Being so close to him was already causing havoc inside her.

She must wind this up. Get Carlo. Go home. But she couldn't resist one more dig because she was hurting so badly.

'So have we all. The difference is that they think they can buy any beautiful thing they want,' she replied in a withering tone.

He looked annoyed by her response. 'Even beauty can be for sale,' he drawled.

Did he mean her? She pruned in her mouth, refusing to give him the last word.

'That's what it comes down to, isn't it?' she snapped, eyes blazing with indignation. 'Houses, paintings, cars, women… they're all trophies to you! I wonder how many people would have chosen an inanimate house over living flesh and blood?'

Dante's eyes darkened with anger. 'If the house is perfect and the flesh and blood has become rotten like your maggot-ridden apple, I imagine few would have difficulty in making a choice,' he shot back.

She flinched, bridling at what he was implying. He thought she'd been drunk that night. It had given him the excuse to leave her. This could be her last chance to put him straight. Before she left him forever, he had to believe her. She'd never been able to bear injustices.

One day he would visit Carlo in England. Dante mustn't ever feed lies to her son and blacken her name. Angrily she slanted her eyes in his direction and said sharply,

'People see what they want to see. You jumped to the wrong conclusion. I was ill, not drunk.' Her mutinous gaze met his and she had to bite her lip to stop herself from shrinking back at his look of disgust. But he was in the wrong, not her. So she tipped up her chin defiantly. 'Have you never admitted to a mistake, Dante?'

'I have never made one,' he growled with force. 'Other than that of marrying you.'

So emphatic. So sure. She shivered. Suddenly she wanted to get Carlo home. Needed her baby safe and sound and away from this megalomaniac.

'You *have* made a mistake. I am determined that eventually you will know the truth.' She drew in a rasping breath. 'But I've had enough of this. I demand to see—'

'You're not in a position to demand anything!' His eyes glittered like black stones and she shivered at his ruthlessness.

Weary of this, hungry for her beloved child's embrace, she muttered tautly, 'I think I am. You need me. You didn't bring me here to discuss the skill of the Severinis in snaffling the most beautiful spot on Lake Como. What exactly do you want?'

'Your cooperation,' he replied. 'Come inside.'

At last! She felt her pulses quicken. Slowly he would unravel his dignity and admit that on consideration he would be magnanimous and let her take Carlo. It was almost inconceivable that he'd confess that he couldn't handle her son without her. He was a proud man. Losing face would be unthinkable. How would he explain away his failure to banish her from Carlo's life?

Keyed up, she allowed herself to be seated in a gloriously comfortable soft kid chair, the arms of which she could not help but stroke. Guiltily she saw Dante watching her, his dark eyes two hot globes of black silk that threatened to make her as malleable as molten metal.

'Tea?' he murmured silkily.

She fumed at the delay. Yet all her senses stupidly sprang

into life in response to his carnal expression. That was how he'd always seen her—as a convenient womb and a sex object.

'Thank you,' she clipped.

He would string this out, just to make her suffer. And there wasn't anything she could do about it.

Restless, impatient, she crossed one long leg over the other. Noticed those mercilessly sensual eyes contemplating their slim, golden length. Felt the stirring of desire again and wondered how on earth she could feel like this when she despised every bone in his body.

It was just a trick of her sexual memory, she told herself bleakly. In time her desperate need for his touch would go. And when that happened she would be cold and emotionless once more—except where Carlo was concerned.

'Carlo,' she said flatly, by way of encouragement.

'Yes. Carlo.'

As if they had all the time in the world, he poured from the silver pot, adding a slice of lemon and placing the almost transparent bone-china cup on a Venetian table beside her, before retiring behind his vast desk. He was utterly in charge of the situation.

She glared at him sitting behind his imposed barrier without expression, her heart leaping so erratically it felt it might burst from her chest.

'Yes?' she felt urged to prompt before she shrieked her impatience like a banshee.

'First, I need to say that Carlo—' he began, and his eyes flicked down to her fingers, which had clenched into white-boned fists.

'Get on with it!' she jerked out, before she could stop herself.

'My apologies. Your time is valuable. I forgot. Carlo,' he said in a gravelly voice, 'is not here.'

Life drained from her body. Suppressing a sob, she lifted her chin and met his simmering gaze full on, her entire body quivering with rage.

'You *rat*! Is this your revenge on me?' she choked, hating him, her eyes bleak and splintered with ice.

'No. I am not that vindictive,' he replied quietly.

When he sipped his tea, she saw to her surprise that his hand was shaking. Fear ripped through her, destroying the carefully erected mask of composure.

'Dear heaven! What's happened to him?' she breathed, her lips parted in fear.

'Afraid of losing your bargaining tool?' he taunted.

'*Is—he—all—right?*' she ground out, her face bleached of colour.

'Fine. I just wanted us to have time to discuss this.'

There was a strange light in his eyes which was almost sexual as he stared at her mouth when it parted in a relieved gasp, and she cringed back in her chair, not trusting him an inch. Her head began to pound with the crackling tension.

'I didn't know, you see,' he explained, 'how long our negotiations would take.'

Negotiations. She felt on firmer ground. Naturally he'd want to ask her for access time.

'They'll take a week,' she said tartly, 'if you continue stalling.'

'So English,' he murmured with a curled lip of distaste. 'So direct.'

'Come to the point,' she insisted, refusing to play his game any longer.

He nodded. '*Allora*. This is the situation.' He leaned back in his chair, watching her steadily with his melted-chocolate eyes, and she felt dizzy as the hysteria rose within her. He must have sensed her desperation because he firmed his lips and continued, 'I need to explain why I have asked you here.'

Her entire body seemed to be turned to ice. This didn't sound good.

'Do,' she managed to snap out.

He scowled and took his time while her heart rate reached alarming levels and the fear made her head spin.

'At first,' he said in unusually rasping tones, 'Carlo was

excited by the journey on the plane and the fun we had in my uncle's Milan apartment where we stayed initially. I gave him my full attention and he loved that.'

'Yes.' Just in time, Miranda restrained herself from saying that it must have been a novelty to have his father's undivided attention. She suspected that sarcasm wouldn't get her anywhere.

'Then when the *palazzo* was ready, we drove here.' Dante gave a faint smile, evidently reliving happy memories. 'He loved his playroom and new toys, the trips on the ferries across the lake...'

He paused, his voice tailing away. She realised that this was distressing him. The oh-so-perfect Dante had discovered that he wasn't enough for his three-year-old son.

She jumped in before she felt sorry for him. 'And then?'

His jaw worked. Pain tore at his mouth. To her surprise, a pang ripped at her chest, though why she should feel any sympathy she couldn't imagine for the life of her.

Very softly he said, 'I regret to say that all my entertaining and affection could not replace the love that he has for you.'

He took a deep breath. Miranda stifled a sudden rush of joyful relief. 'I'm not surprised.'

'I am. But remarkably, despite your poor mothering skills, Carlo is clearly missing you.'

She bit back a wrenching sob so that Dante wouldn't notice how deeply she'd been affected by that last remark. Poor baby, she thought in an agony of despair. They'd never been parted before. Most of his waking hours had been spent with her. He'd been miserable. Had probably cried pitifully...

And suddenly her control snapped. She couldn't hold back her misery, her mind tortured by flashes of cinematic images of Carlo in tears, his small face screwed up in bewilderment and despair.

'Of course he's missing me!' she stormed. 'How could you hurt him like this? You must have known this would happen!'

'But I didn't!' he protested. 'I thought he'd miss his nanny more, since you'd largely abandoned him to her care!'

'Not *true*—!' she gasped.

'I heard different!' he hurled.

Her eyes blazed and she clenched her fists. 'From whom?'

'Someone close to you.'

'The nanny—Susan?'

He shook his head, his black eyes never leaving her tense face. 'Someone else. I know that Carlo rarely saw you—'

'That's a lie!' she spat in outrage.

'I don't think so,' he said tightly. 'I was the only one who gave him any time and affection—'

'Ridiculous! You were never home during those last few months!' she accused.

'An exaggeration!' he retorted. 'Certainly I visited my uncle frequently, because he was ill—'

'And rich!' she goaded.

'However, when I was home,' Dante went on, grimly ignoring her, 'Carlo had my devoted attention. It was obvious that he lacked affection. He clung to me. Wouldn't let me go—'

'Because he felt insecure about you! He never knew when you'd go and when you'd come back—'

'He loves me!' Dante hurled. 'You know he does!'

'Yes,' she agreed coldly. 'But he's precious to me—'

'Because you can use him?'

'I beg your pardon?' she cried in astonishment.

The black eyes were like stones. 'He's good currency,' he said coldly. 'You know I want him—'

'Oh, the Severini heir!' she scathed, fear clutching at her heart. 'We'll see about that.'

'He is my *son*! That's why I want him!' Dante flung in passion and she knew she had a battle on her hands. 'I know you see him as a meal ticket—perhaps, as I said, something to bargain with. Or perhaps as a revenge because your days of sucking me dry are over—'

'Let's get one thing straight,' she said, trying to keep the lid on her temper. 'I don't see Carlo as a means of getting revenge *or* money. He is my child and I love him. I am here to take him home because he needs me. Whatever this…lying *person* says, I am devoted to Carlo. You've seen that for yourself, Dante! Are you blind?'

'You're not particularly demonstrative,' he snapped.

'Are you comparing me with Italian mothers?' she demanded. 'You *know* how I am. I'm not effusive—never have been. I try not to spoil him. But I do hug and kiss him and think of his welfare all the time. I won't have you saying I don't love my own son when it's written in my eyes for anyone to see! I absolutely adore him! I am his *mother*!'

'To my eternal regret.' Dante scowled. 'And I find it inexplicable that he's been asking for you every single day.'

Anguish mingled with delight and longing in her expression. Dante glanced away as if he couldn't bear to look at her.

'Poor little scrap!' she exclaimed, horrified by the trauma Carlo must have suffered. Dante had no option but to realise that she must have custody of their son. Emboldened, she lifted her head belligerently. 'He must have been bewildered when you whisked him off! It's *unbelievable* that you put him through this, Dante!'

'I could hardly leave him with you after what I'd witnessed,' he snarled.

'Me? Supposedly drunk—?'

'If only that were all!' Loathing spilled from his eyes. 'You're a trollop, Miranda. You entertained a man in our bed, knocking back champagne with him and, by the state of you when I arrived, you might have been taking recreational drugs too. While our son lay neglected—'

'None of that's true!' she cried in horror. 'How can you say that—?'

Pain was slashing into every line of his face. 'With great difficulty!' he snarled. 'I know what I saw. You were disorientated and totally out of it. The evidence of your partying, your infidelity, was there for anyone to see—'

'It's an out-and-out lie!' she croaked. 'If that's what you're pretending…'

Dante jerked around, the ferocity of his expression drying

her throat so that she couldn't continue. His face was taut with anger. In his eyes blazed a hatred so intense, so murderous that it was as if he'd stabbed her in the heart.

'Pretending? *Pretending?!*' he cried, in a slicingly cold voice that lashed her more surely than if he'd yelled at her. 'I did not imagine that I came home unexpectedly from Milan and found you virtually comatose, the sheets soaked in champagne, and my son abandoned and screaming his head off in the nursery!' he ripped out. 'You were drugged, drunk and incapable. And from the marks on your body you'd clearly had rough sex with some,' he choked and forced out, 'some common *thug*—'

'*No!* That's a vile lie!' Reliving that evening, she felt as if her head might burst. Everything that had happened was a terrible, sickening blur… 'Of one thing I'm certain!' she cried with passion. 'I've never been unfaithful to you! I've told you that over and over again! I had flu—'

'But no temperature. I checked,' he said stonily.

'I don't care! That's the only explanation—'

'No. Regrettably, it is not.'

'Flu!' she insisted vehemently.

'And champagne is a cure?' he flung. 'In two glasses?'

Her hand strayed to her forehead. She felt nauseous, as she had on that day. Whenever she went to sleep now, she woke up sweating from terrible nightmares in which she seemed to be living out Dante's fantasy that she'd had sex that night. Someone rough and uncaring was ripping off her clothes. Hurling her on the bed. Holding her down.

She blanched. It was true she'd had bruises the next morning. Had that been Dante? she wondered in sudden shock. Taking his revenge?

'Oh, God!' she whispered.

And suddenly her shoulders were being shaken, and she came back to the present time to find the black-eyed Dante standing in front of her and glaring at her in contempt.

She stared at the flare of his jacket where it sat snugly over his slender hips. She must convince him of her innocence.

Find out what he'd done. Then close the matter forever if she was ever to move on and reclaim her life.

'I *don't know* what happened,' she ripped out hoarsely. 'But I swear—'

'Swear all you like. One thing is clear. To this day you have no idea what you were doing,' he said in disgust. 'Do you think that makes it all right?' He sucked in a huge breath. 'There could have been a football team enjoying your favours in your bedroom for all you know! You were too drunk and too drugged to have any idea what was happening!' he exploded.

'I wasn't! None of that is true—!'

'*Yes!* I was there! I saw you, remember?'

He glared down at her with a look that told her he was about to say something significant.

'What…what is it?' she asked shakily.

There was pure loathing in his eyes. 'Surely you realise that under the circumstances,' he snarled, 'I can't *ever* trust you to look after Carlo?'

Horror-struck, she searched his implacable face. The room spun and she gripped the arms of the chair with clawing hands. Chalk-white, she desperately swallowed down the huge lump of emotion that was sitting like a leaden weight in her throat.

'You—you mean…!' Hardly able to breathe, she grabbed the cup and gulped down the still scalding liquid so that she could speak. 'Is that it? Why you've brought me here? To tell me that…I—I can't take Carlo home with me?' she wavered.

The black eyes scorched her into terror-struck silence.

'*Precisely,*' he clipped.

CHAPTER FOUR

LOSING control completely in her misery and anger, Miranda leapt up and slapped his arrogant, smug face, her hand cracking with a sound like a pistol shot.

'You *brute*!' she yelled. Blindly she launched herself at him, beating her fists against his chest. 'You dragged me here, raising my hopes, deliberately taunting me… And all the time you never meant to let me have Carlo! I hate you! Loathe you! You're utterly *contemptible*! He needs me, Dante! You know he does!' she raged. 'My baby needs me and I need him! You promised me I'd see him! You *promised*!'

He grabbed her hands and wrestled them behind her back. He was breathing hard, his nostrils flared and white in contrast to the scarlet marks on his high cheekbones, his perfect white teeth bared in a grimace.

'I know that!' he seethed. 'So this is what whips you into a frenzy! The thought of losing the chance to use Carlo to screw me for half my fortune—!'

'I don't want your money! I don't care about your ill-gotten gains!' she wailed. 'It's Carlo I care about! Punish me all you like, but don't punish a three-year-old child!'

Her body slammed into his with a controlled force. Her upturned face was inches from Dante's grim mouth and she felt a sharp stab of fear at the blazing fury in his coal-black eyes.

'Listen to me!' he snarled. 'I do not intend to give Carlo one more day's distress! How *dare* you think I could hurt him? Why do you think I've swallowed my pride and compromised my honour to bring you over here? I never wanted to see you again. Whenever I think of you and the filth you've been consorting with, my guts scream with pain and disgust! I am ashamed that you have shamed the name of Severini. I wish I didn't have to see you, a shallow, heartless woman who chose to marry purely for material gain—!'

'I *what*? That's absolute rubbish!' she cried in astonishment.

'—and even now you're plotting to make as much as you can from this miserable situation! "Play your cards right"!' he mimicked, aping Lizzie's greedy tone.

She gulped, her heart sinking. 'You've got it wrong!'

'I don't think so. I was warned from the start about you and your motives!'

'Who by?' She quivered with indignation.

'Never you mind. But you aren't what you seem, that I know. You might even be thinking of wheedling your way back into my bed. And, if that fails, you mean to snatch Carlo away and to get yourself a nice, fat divorce settlement—'

'You're mad! Where did you get that idea?'

'From Lizzie's own mouth!'

She froze, her face appalled. The chauffeur! He'd reported Lizzie's remarks…

'Dante!' she choked. 'I—'

'Listen to me!' he growled, giving her a little shake. 'This is a desperate measure for me to take, don't you understand? I am risking everything by doing this! You're a loose cannon—God knows what damage you might do to my son! But I've got to take the risk because he's pining for you.'

She blinked, faltering, trying to understand. Crushed against him, she suddenly became aware of the power he had over her. Power to bend her to his will. Power, also, to arouse her with his hard, male body that burned like a furnace of intense heat against hers. She was consumed by him. Drowning in wanting.

Desperately she tried to keep her mind clear. 'What risk? If I'm not to collect Carlo and take him home, then why on earth have you brought me here?' she stumbled. 'This is a nightmare!' she moaned. Helplessly she gazed up at him. 'I've long since stopped trying to understand you!'

He released her, his eyes glittering with anger behind his

lowered lashes. Yet his lips had curved and parted as if he contemplated kissing her till she couldn't breathe. Awash with his compelling sexuality, she blinked in confusion, trying to make sense of this contradiction. And put it down to his high libido.

'And I, you,' he muttered, his mouth now cruel. 'Pay attention. This is my proposition.'

'You expect me to sleep with you?' she blurted out in panic, knowing she'd shamefully betray her need for him if he ever tried to caress her.

Dante immediately flinched, as though the idea was repulsive. 'You were a little quick to come up with that suggestion,' he taunted. 'Is that what you've been banking on? That sheer lust would drive us together again?'

'N-no!' she husked.

But to her eternal shame her eyes gave the lie to that, and his contemptuous expression told her that he'd recognised the needs of her throbbing body.

'You can forget the idea. I do not touch soiled goods,' he clipped in contempt. 'My standards are above that. I have never understood the need for men to resort to whores.'

'This is the mother of your son you are talking about,' she whispered, appalled that he should regard her in such low esteem.

'And don't I regret that you are!' he snapped, smoothing down his shirt and adjusting his jacket, which had been disarrayed by her frenzied attack. 'Whatever your ice-queen appearance may suggest to the contrary, I know how eager you are for sex. I have personal experience of your wantonness. And your wild outburst just now shows that you are ruled by passions you cannot control—'

'You're denying me my child!' she cried, white-faced and terrified. 'Any woman would go crazy with grief—!'

'Spare me the hearts and flowers,' he snapped. 'I don't buy that one. The trouble is, Miranda, you didn't hear me out. You were too ready to condemn me, to jump to conclusions. You cannot deny that I have Carlo's interests at heart.'

'Only in your own, twisted way,' she retorted sulkily.

He glared. 'I'll ignore that. Unfortunately, where my son's interests are concerned, it seems I have to take you into account.'

The breath left her lungs. She stared at him warily. Yes. He would come up with a solution—and if it included her... Oh, God! What was his Machiavellian mind focused on now?

With a trembling hand she slicked dislodged strands of pale hair back into her chignon, playing for time, for a moment to think.

'Let me know when you are satisfied with your appearance,' Dante drawled, 'and I'll tell you something to your advantage.'

She met his mocking gaze head-on and wished her glare could fell him on the spot. 'Spit it out.'

Italian through and through, he winced at her deliberate choice of phrase. 'Sit,' he snapped, as if talking to a disobedient dog.

Naturally she remained standing. In proud defiance she lifted her chin and drew up the whole slender length of her body. His eyes dropped to her heaving breasts, then the neat, wasp waist. It felt as if he was branding her, the caress of his gaze as it slid over her curving hips forcing her to squeeze her thighs together in an attempt to deny her shameful response.

She only hoped that he couldn't read the signals of her treacherous body. In case he thought she was a pushover, she spoke more forcefully than necessary.

'I won't be bullied—not by you or anybody!' she seethed. Her ice-blue eyes simmered with silvery lights and she lifted her chin high in defiance.

And, thunderously angry for some reason, he turned and walked to the window, his usually liquid movements strangely jerky and uncoordinated. The set of his broad shoulders was daunting, however, and she bit her lip.

That was what he wanted, she thought. To dominate her. To teach her that no one ever crossed him and came away laughing.

Mutinously, she scowled. She hadn't done anything wrong. One day she'd discover what had happened to her that night. And she'd make Dante apologise for doubting her. He'd grovel—she'd see to that!

'Carlo needs you,' he stated in a distant, chillingly frosty voice.

'At least we agree on something,' she said sharply.

'Therefore,' he continued, as if she hadn't spoken, 'I have decided that you will live here.'

Her eyes widened as her jaw dropped. Seconds ticked away before she could jerk out an astonished,

'What?'

In a haughty gesture he swung back on his heel to face her.

'You will have total access to him,' Dante went on as if she hadn't spoken.

'You—you're letting me have him?' she gasped, her face suddenly radiant with hope.

The black eyes flashed and his mouth tightened.

'No.'

She slumped down in the chair, feeling as if he'd hurled a bucket of iced water over her. She passed a shaking hand over the smooth silk of her hair.

'Then what? My patience is exhausted. If you don't tell me exactly what you're proposing,' she grated, 'I'll start smashing things.' With a menacing glare, she picked up a figurine from the desk and held the voluptuous ivory in her cold and trembling hand. 'Starting with this!'

'I'm trying to,' he gritted. 'I am not finding this easy—'

'Do you think I care?' she flung.

His expression became utterly forbidding and closed.

'No,' he answered quietly. 'I don't think you do. Still, at least that will make your part in this less difficult. You will be able to consider this as a business arrangement.'

'A...what?' she gasped.

'We will be colleagues, as we were once before. It worked well then—'

'I was your secretary!' She frowned, puzzled. 'Is that what you want? I am to work for you?'

'Not exactly. I don't think either of us would want the hot-house atmosphere. Me in this chair dictating letters, you sitting there…'

His hoarse rebuttal croaked to a halt. But it had reminded her of the heady days when she was falling in love with him. The way he'd watched her, his dark eyes turning her knees to water, ruining her concentration so that he'd had to come close and go through her shorthand notes, one hand on the back of her chair, his breath whispering on the hairs at the back of her neck.

She gulped and shifted in the seat because of the pooling heat in her loins.

He looked grim, his lips pressed firmly together as though he had loathed the charade he'd had to act out, the pretence of falling in love with his secretary.

Whereas it had been a roller coaster of ecstasy for her. Tense moments of excitement. The thrill of seeing him so cool and businesslike at meetings, knowing they had just made love across his desk…

'What, then?' she jerked out, hurting from the self-torture of those wild memories of unbelievable pleasure.

He took his time to answer, his chest rising and falling several times before he was ready. By which time she hated him for keeping her dangling.

'I propose,' he said tautly, 'that you will live in this house. I want people to assume we are a perfectly normal husband and wife—'

'That's not likely when we're at daggers drawn,' she said caustically.

'They won't know that. Must not know that. To all intents and purposes we will seem to be on good terms,' he snapped. 'For our son's sake we will be polite and courteous to one another in public. We will appear at functions together. It is not necessary that we give an impression that we lust after one another—that would be asking too much of me,' he added scathingly, 'but we will keep up appearances—'

'You must be joking!' she gasped.

'Deadly serious. There will be no bickering, no acid-tipped remarks, and no double meanings in our conversation when Carlo or others are around.'

His eyes were frighteningly remote. Miranda shrank back, absorbing his extraordinary suggestion and the catalogue of dos and don'ts, her face pale with shock.

For several seconds he studied her, then when she said nothing but remained trembling and astonished, he firmed his mouth and continued.

'In your private life,' he said tautly, 'you will be irreproachable. You will not get drunk. You will not take drugs. You will never, *never*,' he roared suddenly, making her jump, 'be indiscreet and cause a scandal by taking a lover. If you do, you're out of here. Is that understood?'

She felt as if he'd hit her with a steam-hammer. He wanted her to live here as his wife. The thought of living with Dante and not making love with him was impossible to imagine.

'You want me to live like a nun for the rest of my life?' she asked slowly.

'Too difficult?' he scorned.

The way things were, she never wanted to commit herself to another man again. Her plush mouth thinned. Stunned and still trying to absorb his suggestion, she pretended indifference.

'I'm just establishing the ground rules.'

'One of which is that you will be chaste and above suspicion. That is my ultimatum. As I said, if you break it, I will throw you out to fend for yourself. And you will never see Carlo again.'

She put a hand to her temple where a pulse throbbed painfully. 'That's why you wanted him out of the way! If I refuse this...gross proposition, then you intend to hide him until I leave! Well, I have no intention of agreeing to your cold-blooded solution. I couldn't possibly live with you! I won't go, either,' she defied. 'I'll stay here until—'

'The police will escort you from the premises,' he stated smoothly.

He smiled faintly when her shoulders dropped, a give-away, she thought in despair, that she was at the end of her tether.

'Maybe. But I won't go quietly! I'll raise hell!' she threatened.

'Then everyone will sympathise with me about the fishwife I mistakenly married,' he flung back. 'Your attitude would affect your chances of access. Besides, no one will believe anything you say. I will reveal my reasons for keeping you from Carlo and the courts will uphold my request for sole custody. You will be deported as an undesirable.'

Her eyes darkened to violet. Now she was clutching at straws, searching for anything to fight him with. Tears welled up as she thought of Carlo's unhappiness and she racked her brains for a way to gain mastery over Dante.

'In that case, I will walk away quietly,' she amended, 'and stay near by. People will murmur and wonder why my son is so sad and why I stand at your gates hoping for a glimpse of him!' she hurled.

His jaw set hard. 'You have no money, Miranda. How will you survive? Or…is that a silly question when your assets are clearly displayed before me?'

'You are obsessed with whoring!' she yelled in frustration, hating the fact that he was right about her poverty and seeing no way out but to surrender. In one final stab, she snapped, 'Strange that you were perfectly happy for me to play the whore for you in bed!'

'And anywhere else, for that matter. You did it so well,' he murmured, so mockingly sexy that her breath began to jerk in the furnace of her body. 'But those days are over. And I find it interesting that you see your role in that light. I fondly imagined you were enjoying uninhibited sex with the man you loved. But of course, you had sold yourself to me, hadn't you?'

The look in his eyes belied his remark that their physical relationship had ended. A desperate and unstoppable desire heated the air between them. Hunger was in every tense inch of his body. She had seen it too often before to doubt the evidence of her own eyes. He wanted her.

As much—heaven help her—as she wanted him. They were still physically tied and it would take a while before their passion for one another waned. The memories were too recent, too intense, and too ecstatic.

She felt hot, the electrically charged atmosphere swamping her senses. It took a huge effort of will to reject his unspoken invitation. Yet she must, because otherwise he'd destroy her.

There was something more important to consider. Carlo. She had no doubt that Dante would carry out all his threats. It seemed she had no choice.

'If—*if*—I should agree to your disgusting plan,' she croaked, 'then I'd want your guarantee that you won't touch me.'

How odd. Immediately after she'd made this stipulation she felt miserable…*empty*, at the thought of never reconciling with Dante. After all, she'd never be able to trust him again. Or to respect him. She sighed. Bodies were odd things—totally *at* odds with one's brain.

Dante's intake of breath broke the spell and he seemed to withdraw into himself, his head lifting proudly.

'I would rather kiss a cockroach,' he drawled.

She flinched at his vile insult. 'The feeling's mutual.' Or it would be, once she'd got over him. 'Let's get something straight,' she said with dignity. 'I was ill when you abandoned me that night. I could have been *seriously* ill for all you knew. In fact it took days before I felt better. Not only did you take our son away—although I'd looked after him devotedly—'

'That's debatable—'

'Devotedly!' she emphasized. 'But you scuttled away and secreted yourself away somewhere, too afraid to face me. Those are the actions of a heartless, callous man. Someone who is an abject coward, Dante! And to think I once believed you were hero material! Huh!' she scorned. 'I despise you. How could I possibly be polite to you when I feel hatred and loathing and contempt for you?'

His shoulders hooked up in a shrug but she could see from the tautness of his mouth that her words had struck home.

'You must realise that I had to remove Carlo from you,' he said in a choked tone, his eyes lowered so that she could not see if they were pained. 'I had to give him a chance to be without you and your malign influence. I didn't like doing it— and I don't like doing *this*, Miranda. But for his sake, I must. Maybe I can wean him from you. I don't know. But as sure as hell, you will never be alone with him!'

So he'd make her play his game of happy families—and then get rid of her! No way.

And yet he'd acted in good faith. He'd thought he was doing the right thing where Carlo was concerned. That did alter her opinion of him a little. And so she tried another tack, giving him a chance to salvage his pride and admit he'd been wrong to think he could bring up Carlo.

'Dante. I realise this must be hard for you,' she began more evenly.

'Hard? That is an understatement,' he muttered, his gaze fixed grimly on his glove-soft shoes.

'For the moment, we can't agree about what happened that evening,' she went on, trying to stay level-headed. His suggestion was unworkable. He must see that. 'But we can agree about one thing: Carlo's best interests. You love him. And you know in your heart of hearts that he'll be happier with me in England—'

'Until you neglect him again and then he'll be miserable!' Dante exploded. 'I can't let you have him! I'd never sleep. I'd go out of my mind with worry!'

His anguish was genuine. He really cared about Carlo and, because he believed she'd been selfish and promiscuous while he was on business trips, he was trying to protect his son. That was laudable—if misguided. Carlo didn't need protecting from her.

'I promise you—' she began fervently.

'No! I will not risk my son's happiness on the promise of a woman I don't trust and who has deceived me all down the line! That is my final word!' Dante snapped.

He was convinced that he was justified in his actions. Like her, he would die for their child. Dante would not waver in his determination, she knew him too well.

They were going round in circles. Wearily she passed a hand over her aching head. Lack of sleep and food, the constant tension as she had hunted for Dante in his commercial outlets around Europe, had taken their toll. She was close to giving in. It would be easier than this constant fighting...

'Let's explore your suggestion. Supposing I agreed,' she said, her voice shaking with exhaustion. 'What is your intention? That I would live here, in a room of my own?'

'Not exactly. You would have your own apartments but you would reach them from my suite of rooms to avert scandal and gossip. The young woman I have in mind for your personal maid is a distant cousin. She can be trusted not to divulge any secrets of our sleeping arrangements. You would, in effect, be alone. And let me say that if you are tempted to try your luck with me, you'll find a padlock the size of a dinner plate on my side of the door,' he added scathingly.

She flushed. 'I'm relieved to hear that. We can both stick to kissing cockroaches! One more thing. If I did come to stay, I would want to earn my own living,' she stipulated. 'As a secretary,' she added, seeing where his vile mind was heading.

He looked down his nose at her. 'The wife of a count does not work.'

'A *count*!' she exclaimed. 'My, my, we have come up in the world. I wouldn't stand a chance if I took you to court, would I?'

'Not a hope.'

She stared at him, suddenly crushed by his loathing and the prospect of living a lie.

'I couldn't do it!' she whispered.

'Not for Carlo? Then do it for the life of luxury,' he said

coldly. 'You will have a generous allowance and a credit card, the bills for which I will pay. I will make provision for you in my will, in the event of my death. On the condition that—'

'I behave like a nun.'

He bowed his head in acknowledgement. 'A woman of impeccable morality will do.'

All of a sudden she wanted to be free of him. Of his overwhelming presence, his suffocating dominance. The occasional drifts of vanilla fragrance she recognised which clung discreetly to his body, and which she had once inhaled with joyous delight as her mouth had explored every inch of him. All this was clouding her senses, making her head whirl.

'I'd be mad to agree! You would have a terrible hold over me,' she muttered. 'You could manipulate everything I did—'

'Forget what's gone between us. Think of our son. All I want is for him to feel secure and happy.' He pushed his hands into his trouser pockets, looking worried. 'If you love him, as you say you do, then surely you want that too? You see, Miranda, I will never let him go. He belongs here. This is his heritage, his right. A glorious future. Would you deny him that?'

'He needs to be loved more than he needs material wealth—' she began shakily.

'He will be loved!' Dante snapped.

'In a coldly polite atmosphere that will surround his parents?'

He folded his arms, his eyes blazing at the prospect of being thwarted.

'If you come here, I am sure we would both do our utmost to put the past behind us and make the best of this mess. It's the only way, Miranda, believe me. I've spent hours pacing up and down thinking of a solution. This is the only one I can live with.'

She bit her lip, wavering. It sounded so simple, the way he put it. Cut and dried. And horribly emotionless. She'd never known him to be so cold and remote.

'I don't know... I need time. I want to be alone, to think this over.'

His face darkened. 'What is there to think about? Personally, I would give up everything for my son.'

His criticism was plain. 'Then let me have a small house here and bring him up—' she began eagerly.

'No!' He looked shocked. 'I couldn't trust you to care for him properly. Besides, Carlo will inherit from me. The business. The silk mills, the outlets, the offices around the world. This estate. The flat in Milan, the villa on the Veneto and the house in Antigua. To say nothing of the fortune behind it all. He needs to know how to handle wealth. How to run the business—'

'He's only three!' she wailed, stunned by the extent of Dante's inheritance. Suddenly she felt out of her depth. Dante had the whip hand.

'And if he grows up here, he will learn naturally how to deal with people. He will learn that power brings responsibility and carries with it a sense of duty,' Dante snapped. 'One day he will be Il Conte Severini. He must not shame the name and blunder about helplessly because he doesn't know how to behave. Or do you want your son to be disinherited and for my brother, Guido, to take his place?'

She shuddered at the mention of Guido's name but didn't know why. There was a foul taste in her mouth suddenly. All her instincts were railing against Guido inheriting Carlo's birthright.

'You're asking a lot of me. Let me think,' she said weakly. '*Please!* It's such an important step. We'd be committed to living a lie for the rest of our lives!'

It seemed a prison sentence. But she knew in her heart of hearts that she would do anything for her child...even this, if she could come up with no other solution.

Her head ached. Frowning, she rubbed at her temple, knowing she needed privacy to work things out. To come to terms with her frightening future.

Slowly she lifted her head and gazed at Dante with huge,

tear-washed eyes, her mouth trembling with misery and fatigue.

He seemed remote, the honeyed skin taut over his cheek-bones, his lips no longer curved in a sensual arch but pressed into a hard, grim line. He would never relent, she thought in desperation, and felt like weeping at her defeat.

'Please, Dante! Give me time!' she whispered again.

There was no indication in his face that he recognised this, not even when two huge, crystal teardrops squeezed from each corner of her eyes. As she saw his stony expression, the granite of his jaw, her whole body drooped. She was hanging on by a thread and he didn't give a damn.

'As you wish,' he said in an uncharacteristic rasp. Perhaps he was angry that she hadn't agreed immediately, and was trying to conceal his rage, she thought dully. 'Perhaps some fresh air will help. I will show you the way to the garden, where you can consider my offer. You've got an hour. No longer.'

Again that jerky walk. A shaking hand on the doorknob that betrayed his tension. Puzzled, she wondered just how badly Dante wanted to 'keep up appearances'. Presumably it had been pointed out to him that it was not proper for him to be married and to live apart from his wife. Maybe the Italian aristocracy would frown on divorce.

If so, she thought tiredly, following him down the stairs, she had a small advantage. Perhaps she could push through some alterations to his ruthless plan...

'Darling!'

Already heading for the back of the hall, they both whirled at the trilling cry. Miranda saw that the tall, elegant figure of Dante's mother stood in the open doorway, framed against the sunlight, her arms held out in a typically generous welcome.

'Sonniva!' Miranda said in surprise. And to her horror, she gave a little choking cry.

'My dear! Oh, you poor darling!' crooned Sonniva, clacking rapidly across the chequered marble.

And then Miranda was enveloped in silken arms, the birdlike body grasping her with surprising energy, two gentle hands stroking and soothing her as if she were a child.

'*O, povera piccolina!* You poor little one! How glad I am to see you,' Dante's mother murmured, great wafts of Paradiso perfume drifting enticingly into Miranda's senses. 'It must have been so hard, being in an isolation hospital and not allowed to see your own husband and child! I'm thrilled you're better now. But you look so thin!' she chided, taking Miranda's startled face between her palms. 'And pale! Dante! She is still not well. We must look after you. Red wine and chocolates, yes?' She lowered her voice to a whisper. 'The fever. All is well now? The hospital has let you go and you are here to stay?'

She took a deep breath, feeling wrecked. Her eyes slipped to Dante. She was shocked to see how alarmed he looked. So that was the story—that she'd been in hospital with a dangerously contagious illness. What a liar he was!

'Miranda, darling!' crooned Sonniva in concern. 'You look…how do I say it?….*dazed*. Dante, she is staying, isn't she? Oh, he's been such a bear without you! And I couldn't bear little Carlo to cry so pitifully for his *mama* again!'

'You're exaggerating, Mama—' Dante began.

But the damage was done. 'Oh, dear heaven!' Miranda whispered, utterly broken by Sonniva's final sentence. She drew in a shuddering breath. 'Yes. Yes. I'm staying.'

Dante's relief was palpable. She was aware of the relaxing of his muscles, one by one, and knew that she must do everything in her power to prove to him that she had been wrongfully accused. Or her life would be an utter hell.

CHAPTER FIVE

'I WILL collect Carlo for you,' Sonniva said decisively. 'Dante has done his best to be a mother and father while you've been in hospital, you can be sure, Miranda. He has been so attentive, so loving to our little darling. To cheer him up today, Dante arranged a little entertainment after nursery—a trip on the train, a fun party with some friends and a garden full of...*come si dice*?' she asked, turning to the impassive Dante.

'Bouncy castles and play equipment,' he provided. 'Thank you, Mama. I'd be glad if you will collect him from his friends in Cadenabbia. Miranda will have a chance to rest before Carlo returns.'

'And you two can be together. What a thrill for you! *Allora*. You can "rest" with her, Dante, yes? But don't exhaust her. See you in a while, darlings.'

With her eyes twinkling mischievously, Sonniva blew kisses and breezed out.

'Thank you,' Dante said hoarsely.

'For what? Helping you to lie to your own mother? How low will you stoop, Dante?' she asked with contempt.

'For my son, I will do anything,' he muttered.

Yes. She had the impression he would. She leaned tiredly against a marble pillar, her head feeling as if it might burst.

'So I have discovered. How long before Carlo is here?'

'My mother will drive to the car ferry to cross the lake, then it's a short drive to my friend's house. By the time she's eased Carlo from the party and made the return trip...say an hour or a little longer.'

She nodded. 'I do need a few moments to myself. I'd like to lie down. Where can I crash out?'

'Your bedroom—'

'No,' she said decisively. 'I'd never wake up. Somewhere comfortable where I can curl up in an armchair.'

'The library, then,' he said at once. 'No one will disturb you there and you can use the sofa. Shall I—?'

'No!' He had extended an arm, as if to support her. She shrank from his touch and said stiffly, 'Point me in the right direction.'

'Of course.'

At least he seemed to have realised that she'd scream if he pawed her, or scolded her any more. She badly needed to be left in peace for a while, to chew over what she'd taken on.

But she stumbled and his hand shot out to stop her from falling. For a moment she hovered dangerously close to him, every cell in her body begging her to fall into his arms, and then he was pushing her along impatiently as if he, too, wanted nothing more than to be free and alone.

Then, somewhere in the distance, she heard a high-pitched voice she recognised.

'Lizzie!' She groaned in dismay.

'I'll deal with her. She can stay the night then I'll put her on the next flight back first thing in the morning.'

'I should speak to her...' Miranda chewed her lip guiltily. 'I'll need to explain—'

'Leave a note,' he advised. 'Let me handle her. If I stuff money into her bag I'm sure she'll be co-operative. I'll get Guido to meet her flight in London. He'll smooth things over.'

Miranda winced at his contempt for Lizzie but knew he was right. And she really couldn't face her sister. Later she'd invite her over and give her a nice time.

'Thank you,' she whispered, and allowed herself to be led into the library, where she scrawled a hasty note and handed it to Dante.

Her gaze scanned the walls of books, tiers upon tiers of them in carved bookshelves, which stretched right up to the high, carved ceiling. The volumes were nearly all leather-bound and were probably valuable antiques.

It seemed that every detail of the house underlined Dante's

newly acquired wealth and power. Everywhere she looked—the gilded furniture, fine porcelain, the crystal chandeliers, the frescoed ceiling—she discovered further evidence of the Severini heritage. And Carlo would own this one day.

Her job would be to keep him human. Normal. To know more than this world with its rarefied atmosphere. Yes. She had an important role to play. And Dante had better accept that.

She reached the soft cream sofa and her body sank into its welcoming depths with relief. Pulling a handful of silk cushions towards her, she arranged them comfortably behind her aching back and kicked off her shoes.

Without a word, Dante poured her a glass of water from a crystal decanter, handed it to her, then walked quietly away, shutting the heavy oak door behind him. Leaving her in the hushed, muffled silence.

Now she could flop. Every bone in her body felt as if it might crack. Her muscles ached from being held in tension. Limply she raised a hand and lightly massaged her forehead, then held the cold glass against her throbbing temples.

What a dramatic turn her life had taken! It was almost unbelievable. She was to live here, to all intents and purposes the count's wife. *La contessa!*

Her eyes closed in dismay. Acting out a charade would be hard enough, but to be isolated in a foreign country…

'Heaven help me!' she whispered. 'Give me strength, for Carlo's sake!'

She quailed at the daunting prospect. To enable her to cope she would negotiate her own rules with Dante. Invite friends over. Make a life of her own.

Dante would *not* rule her with an iron fist. Carlo must see at first hand that marriage was a partnership. The last thing she wanted was for her own son to see her as inferior—or for him to grow up with the same attitude to women as his father.

She vowed that Carlo would learn that women were to be treated with respect. That they must be loved for their individuality and not treated as a convenience.

She made a wry face. What was she doing? He was only just three years old! And yet, she thought more soberly, he would undoubtedly pick up his future attitudes from the cradle.

Her teeth snagged at her lip. When Carlo had been spirited away, he'd had a sweet and loving nature. She prayed that he hadn't suffered any long-term damage and that they could rebuild any feelings of abandonment and insecurity.

Given Dante's total commitment, they probably could. She would talk to Dante and they'd draw a line under the past two weeks. In Carlo they had a combined interest. They could live a civilised life. They must, for their son's emotional well-being.

Thinking of her son's small, sunny face, she gave a blissful smile. 'Oh, my darling!' she whispered passionately. 'See you soon, very soon!' And with her nerves calmed by this reassuring thought, she drifted off to sleep.

It was dark when she woke. A small glow of light from the moon silvered the gleaming marble floor so that it looked like a vast lake.

Immediately she sat up in alarm. Night? The luminous dial on her watch told her it was ten o'clock.

Her entire body froze. She'd slept for four hours. And Dante had not kept his promise to bring Carlo to her! She let out a wail of dismay.

Without stopping to put on her shoes, she ran through the faintly lit room and into the corridor that led to the hall, her hair falling from its pins and flying loose around her frantic face like a silky white curtain.

'Dante!' she yelled in fury and panic. 'Dante!'

There came the sound of a man's feet, running. The door to a brightly lit room burst open and Dante came hurrying out, frowning deeply.

'Miranda! Hush! What is it?' he demanded, coming to a sudden halt a foot away from her.

'Carlo!' she jerked brokenly and could say nothing else.

At the mention of his son's name, his features softened.

'Asleep. Do you want to see him?' he asked in an almost gentle tone.

Emotion had claimed her vocal cords. Mutely she nodded, her eyes huge and misty.

'I thought… I thought…' she said, sounding strangled.

'I know,' he said tightly. 'Thanks for the vote of confidence.'

'If you're playing a trick on me, I'll make you sorry you were born!' she muttered.

He grimaced. 'I'm sure you would.'

'Why didn't you wake me?' she demanded fretfully as he led her to the grand staircase.

'There was no point,' Dante explained stiffly. 'After the hours of activity and excitement, he fell asleep in my mother's car on the way back.'

'That's no reason not to wake me! I wouldn't have cared! Just to see his face…'

The words became choked with disappointment and she had to stop.

'I did come in to tell you he was home,' he said quietly. 'But you looked very peaceful in your sleep. You were—' he frowned '—smiling. And yet you had an air of exhaustion. I did not have the heart to wake you. I'm sorry if it was the wrong decision, but my mother agreed that another night wouldn't make much difference, and that both of you needed to rest.'

'Because of my illness,' Miranda muttered mutinously, sweeping her hair behind her ears.

She trembled a little. It gave her an odd feeling to know that he'd watched her sleeping.

'I'm sorry about that, I should have warned you about the story I'd invented to cover your absence, but I wasn't expecting Mama to turn up,' he explained. 'When I left England so unexpectedly with Carlo I didn't know what to tell her—or anyone else for that matter. I couldn't bring myself to reveal the truth.' His face darkened. 'Whatever happened, I didn't want our child to discover one day how badly you had behaved. So I lied while I worked out what to do for the best.'

'You didn't lie to your chauffeur.' She looked him directly in the eye.

'How do you know that?'

'The way he treated me. Without respect.'

'I will speak to Luca. My chauffeur,' Dante said quietly.

'Do that. What exactly did you tell him?' she demanded.

'The bare minimum. Luca drove Carlo and me from Malpensa—Milan Airport—after...after I found you that evening,' Dante replied in a low tone. 'He knew I was in a terrible state. Kept Carlo amused with songs and stories. Fed me coffee and brandy, bought a toy for Carlo at the service station on the *Autostrada* to entertain him. Somehow I let slip that you'd been unfaithful.'

'Dante! How could you?' she cried in dismay.

He frowned. 'He is one of the few I trust—apart from Guido, of course—who wouldn't dream of tarnishing the family honour with any revelations. As far as Luca is concerned, I wish I'd kept my mouth shut, but I wasn't in full possession of my senses,' he said tightly. 'But he'll say nothing, for my sake. His father worked for mine. Luca has been my European driver since he left school and is totally loyal and reliable. He won't even have said anything to his wife. You can be sure of that.'

And she'd speak to Luca, too, she vowed. Put her side of the story.

Dante opened a massive carved door at the top of the stairs and politely stood to one side in a gesture that still made her feel cherished. Luca forgotten, Miranda smiled in anticipation, her eyes searching the darkened room within as she stepped breathlessly into the room. Dante softly closed the door behind them.

A small lamp glowed by the bed, its soft light illuminating...

She frowned, staring at the vast canopied four-poster, elaborately decorated. Rich brocade hangings.

Her senses alerted, she quickly scanned the bedroom. It was very masculine, despite the elegant eighteenth-century furniture. Seeing Dante's honey-coloured silk robe on a chair, she stopped breathing.

No sign of Carlo. This wasn't a child's room at all. Almost certainly it belonged to Dante himself. And why would he bring her to his bedroom…?

In a fury she whirled around. 'You rat! Let me out—!'

She didn't finish the sentence. Dante had caught her arms in warning.

'Be quiet!' he whispered fiercely. 'You'll wake him!'

Before she could gather her wits, she found herself being pushed towards the bed. Her head whirled. She felt strangely dizzy. It was as if she were in a time warp; those hands holding her—though she remembered them as being more brutal—and a sense of being trapped and helpless…

'There! Now will you believe me?' Dante muttered.

Despite the rising terror, she blinked away the fog and focused. The fear vanished in an instant when she saw the dark head of her sleeping child.

'Carlo!' she whispered. Dante released her. She ran to the bed and knelt in a fever of joy. 'Oh, my darling, I've missed you!' she breathed, somehow holding back her intense longing to catch up her son and crush him in her arms. He looked utterly content, the long black lashes settling thickly on his baby cheeks, the rosebud mouth pursed in sleep. 'Mummy's here,' she said, choked. Maybe in his dreams he'd hear what she was saying. 'Mummy's come back.'

Tentatively she reached out an alarmingly shaky hand and touched the chubby little arm clad in the dinosaur pyjamas with dinosaur buttons which she'd bought for him shortly before he'd disappeared. Carlo sighed and then he smiled his creamy smile.

Speech was beyond her. Miranda's own face lit up with a soft radiance because she imagined that he really did know she was close by. And her heart melted completely when his mouth began making little sucking noises as if he were still at her breast.

Gently she replaced the covers, which Dante had drawn back so that she could see her son. Carlo snuggled into them, his dark head almost disappearing. From a few feet away it would be hard to know he was there.

With loving motions she smoothed the oyster silk bedspread and hungrily watched her son sleeping. She was filled with happiness, with choking emotion, with uncontainable love.

Two weeks. It had been an eternity. Days, hours, minutes, seconds of interminable misery. But they would not be parted again. Dante had promised...

Remembering him, she looked around. He was watching her, his dark eyes silvery from the reflected light of the moon. For a moment it almost seemed as though they were full of tears but she knew it was an illusion when he growled in a surly tone,

'I think I'm owed an apology.'

Her eyes widened and she rose unsteadily to her feet.

'Why?'

'You thought I'd brought you to my room to seduce you. Or do you think I might have tried rape?' he grated.

Her elation faded and she bit her lip. She pushed her hand through her tumbling curtain of hair, trying to tidy it.

'You're right. I'm sorry. I panicked when I realised this was your room. It never occurred to me that Carlo would be here. It only goes to show how little I trust you, doesn't it?' she finished sadly. 'Why is he in your bedroom, anyway?'

He stalked to the door and motioned for her to leave. Once outside, he launched into a tightly controlled explanation.

'Carlo wouldn't sleep on his own. Each night he stayed up with me, constantly asking when you were coming home. He would only fall asleep if I held him in my arms. If I put him in a bed of his own he knew, even in his sleep, that he wasn't being cuddled and he'd wake up yelling.'

Miranda flinched. 'Poor darling! He knew something was wrong—'

'Do you think I don't know that?' Dante said tightly. 'Do you think it didn't tear me apart? I couldn't bear his misery. I began to take him into my own bed when I retired for the night. Now he's happy to sleep there without me because he feels secure in it. In time I hope he'll go to his own room. But for now, he needs love, Miranda!' he added angrily. 'He's been starved of it, poor child—'

'That's absolute rubbish! Don't you dare to accuse me without proof!' she cried, close to breaking point.

And to her dismay, the world seemed to whirl around and she swayed unsteadily on her feet.

'*Che Dio mi aiuti!*' he swore, his strong hands immediately steadying her. 'No more of this. You need to eat. It's past ten o'clock and you have hardly eaten anything all day, I imagine.'

Miranda tried to remember. 'I had coffee,' she began. But could think of nothing else. She'd been too churned up to swallow a thing.

'As I thought,' he said with irritation. 'No wonder you can hardly stand. Come down and eat with me.'

She shrank from the idea and the memories it aroused. Sometimes they had fed one another. And they had gone on to satisfy other, more urgent appetites.

'It's late. I'm tired,' she demurred, afraid of her weakness, of the hold he had over her senses. 'I'll be fine when I get to bed—'

'Do you want to be well tomorrow?' he demanded. 'To play with Carlo? To have some energy? *D'accordo.* You will eat something. I insist.'

She capitulated suddenly, realising that he was right. And discovered to her surprise that she was very hungry indeed. 'Yes. I will. Now I've seen Carlo,' she said, her face becoming soft and tender with motherly love, 'I think I could eat for England.'

Dante said nothing but his hands dropped from her arms abruptly and he turned away from her, his expression stone-hard. Her happiness evaporated in the teeth of his hatred and she vowed again to prove her innocence—though how, she couldn't imagine.

As they descended the stairs she felt alarmingly woozy from lack of food and too much caffeine, and grabbed the gleaming banister. She sensed an instinctive movement of Dante's hand in her direction and then its withdrawal. He was very tense and she wondered why.

The meal was conducted in total silence apart from the scrape of silver forks on plates and the soft background music Dante liked during dinner.

Miranda concentrated on assuaging her hunger with an artistically arranged antipasto of Parma ham, pâté, pasta and diced vegetables, then prawns in raspberry vinegar followed by cheese and fruit. It was the kind of food which would once have pleased all her senses but Dante's cold indifference ruined her enjoyment and turned it into nothing other than a necessary fuel for the body.

The vintage wine, however, gradually made her feel as if all her muscles were oozing into her melting bones. Flushed and bright-eyed, with her hair tumbling about her face, she popped the last grape into her mouth and wiped her fingers on the soft napkin.

'I'll turn in now,' she said quietly, wondering how many silent dinners she'd have to endure over the coming years. Unusually emotional, she blinked and swallowed before she was able to add, 'Perhaps you'd show me my room.'

He looked up and their eyes met. His frown smoothed out and was replaced by a longing so deep and visceral that she caught her breath, her lips parting and swelling. She had discarded her jacket and knew that the silk of her cream camisole was suddenly tight where her breasts had bloomed into new life.

She couldn't speak, dared not move, and could only stare at him helplessly and hope that her stupid desire for him would vanish in time. Preferably during the next few seconds.

She took a deep breath and realised that she had innocently drawn Dante's dark, hot eyes back to her straining breasts.

The atmosphere thickened and became suffocating. The pool of heat between her legs intensified. The magic was still there. For both of them. In her fantasy, they'd fall into one another's arms and he would declare that he'd loved her all along and his uncle's inheritance was purely a coincidence...

'Go into my bedroom, turn right through the double doors into the adjoining apartment. I'll lock the doors when I come up in a moment,' he rasped.

It was as if he'd slapped her. He knew full well that she was aroused. The cynical curl of that sensuous mouth told her that. And because he believed her to be soiled goods, he was determined not to give way to his own desire. Or even to do the gentlemanly thing and escort her to her room.

Humiliated and struggling for composure, she stalled until she felt certain she could walk away with dignity.

'Fine. And what time does Carlo wake?' she asked coolly.

'About seven.'

'Will you be dressed by then?' she enquired.

'If the door's unlocked, I'll be dressed.'

'I'll knock, just in case,' she said tartly, and she rose to her feet and stalked out, her heart breaking.

CHAPTER SIX

'MIRANDA! Miranda!'

She was being shaken. Crying in fright, she fought her assailant and this time, *this time,* instead of being unable to move a muscle, she found her fists connecting with flesh.

This, too, had happened before, she thought. And sickness rose in her throat adding to the terror.

'Get off me! Get off me!' she screamed instinctively, utterly disorientated.

A hand clapped over her mouth—again. Please, sweet heaven, not again!

Normally her eyes stayed stubbornly shut during her nightmares, but now they snapped open. The light was on in her adjoining sitting room, allowing her to see Dante bending over her, his robe hanging loose to show his bare torso above pale gold pyjama bottoms.

'Keep the noise down!' he hissed.

She cringed. Was this what had happened on that fateful evening? Dante assaulting her, she fighting him off…

Groggy from sleep, not fully alert, she lashed out, her arms and legs pummelling him unmercifully. But he resisted, taking the blows with a wince and leaning unnervingly close.

'*Santo cielo!* How often must I say that I have no intention of raping you.' he grated in her ear. 'You shouted out in your sleep. Began to scream. You've had a nightmare, Miranda. Now calm down. I don't want Carlo disturbed. I know you have a sitting room between here and my bedroom but you were yelling fit to wake the dead!'

Her enormous sapphire eyes stared up at his icily angry face as she came to full consciousness. Yes. It had been that awful recurring dream again. Her tense body went limp and he removed his hand.

In misery, she squeezed her eyes tight shut. Would she never be free of her nightmare? It came relentlessly night after night and she almost feared going to sleep, knowing that some time she would wake as she had now, bathed in sweat and shaking with a terror of something unknown.

'Cover yourself up,' he said curtly and in the dim light she saw to her embarrassment that one sleepy-nippled breast had escaped from her low-cut black satin nightdress.

As she scrambled to draw the covers up to her chin, she shivered, the perspiration cooling on her heated skin.

'I'm so cold!'

The grim-faced Dante turned away and strode to the door. 'I'll get you a brandy.'

'Don't leave me!' she cried desperately before she could stop herself.

He stopped dead, his back still to her, fists clenched at his sides. Spoke in a low and husky tone.

'What is it, Miranda? You never used to have dreams like this.' He jerked his head around to look at her. 'Have you been involved in something dark and unpleasant—or with someone who's taken you to depths you wish you'd never known?'

'No! Nothing like that!' she whispered, still in shock from the experience.

'Something must have caused this! You were frantic. Hysterical.' His eyes went cold and hard and his voice shook with fury. 'This is what comes of living dangerously! Inviting God knows who back to our home—'

'No—!'

'Drinking, taking drugs—'

'*No—!*'

'And not knowing what the hell happened next!' he grated, his mouth twisted in disgust. 'How *could* you put our son at risk—?'

'I didn't! I didn't!' she cried piteously. 'I wouldn't, honestly, not in a million years—!'

'You've no idea what you did!' he fumed. 'And I don't know how many times it had happened before. I can't believe you could be so stupid, so irresponsible—'

'I wasn't!' she moaned, her hands covering her face.

His accusations were making her feel worse. She fought to control the waves of nausea as they rolled through her gut and rose to her throat. But she couldn't defend herself any more because she was unable to speak or to stop the violent shaking. Her teeth chattered and the lines of his mouth flattened out with irritation.

'Maledizione!' he muttered.

And in a moment she was being encircled by warm, comforting arms. Held to a naked chest in which a heart beat with such force that it sounded like a rapid drumbeat. The faint rasp of stubble on Dante's jaw settled firmly against her cheek and he was murmuring soothing words in Italian as if she were a frightened child.

She gave in to her needs. Put her arms around his neck and crushed him hard against her.

'Please,' she whispered helplessly. 'Stay with me!'

Dante groaned. She took his face in her hands to plead with him and found her mouth opening invitingly, her eyes lowering drowsily as she contemplated the incredibly sensual arch of his lips.

'I don't think so,' he said, seething with barely controlled anger. With almost indecent haste he pulled away. 'I won't go far. I'll get you some water instead,' he snapped curtly, standing up and striding to the bathroom. 'And a towel to wipe your face. You'll feel better then.'

He continued to talk even when she couldn't see him, his tones losing their rasping quality and becoming more matter-of-fact as if she were a fractious child to be soothed.

'...and then we can both get some sleep,' he was saying in a nannying tone when he re-emerged. 'Here.'

He thrust a hand towel at her and she obediently used it to

wipe the beads of perspiration that had broken out all over her face and throat. But her hand shook too much to hold the glass of water. Dante held it to her lips and frowned as she took small, nervous sips.

'Are you coming off drugs? Is that the reason for the bad dreams, your loss of weight and this uncontrollable trembling?' he demanded with a sudden harsh suspicion.

'How can you think that?' she cried in horror.

'You show all the classic signs. I warn you, Miranda,' he snarled, his face close to hers, 'if you ever let any illegal substances get within snorting distance of this house, you'll be on the next flight to England before you know it. Carlo will never see you again—nor will he ever want to! You'll be wiped from our lives as if you never existed!'

'I've never taken any drugs! Never would in a million years!' she choked out. 'I had a nightmare, that's all. But it was horrible!' she muttered, shuddering. Her eyes grew enormous, and thinking of it, she began to breathe fast with fear, hating the feeling of helplessness in her dream. 'So horrible that I daren't sleep!' she blurted out. 'It'll come back again if I do, I know it.'

Dante frowned. 'This is not like you to be so negative and defeatist.'

'I know! But this isn't any ordinary nightmare, Dante! I live every vile, terrifying second. Someone is assaulting me and I can't raise a finger to stop it even though every sense is intensified. I smell bad breath. I taste something foul. I feel...'

She clammed up. Would not tell him of those rough, hurting hands. And the frightening blank in her mind that came next. That was even worse and it fed her imagination in ways she didn't want to know. But he had seen in her face the extent of her horror because he said gruffly,

'Take it easy. Maybe you've learnt your lesson and it's over—'

'That's the trouble!' she jerked in despair. 'It isn't. It returns to haunt me even in the daytime. And comes back night after night.'

A little more of the dream unfolded each time. One day maybe the whole horrific event would reveal itself—and she dreaded that more than anything.

His expression was bleak. 'Relax,' he advised tautly. 'Don't try to relive it. You have to forget it.'

If only she could! She closed her eyes in misery and felt his hand cover hers, stilling its trembling in an instant. He had the ability to make her feel secure. Even if it was an illusion.

'Thank you,' she said, with a grateful glance at his harrowed face. 'I feel safe with you. No, please!' she protested when he made to draw his hand away.

'Be realistic. I can't stay, can I?' he said, not unkindly.

But she gripped his wrist to stop him leaving, overwhelmed by an illogical sense of hysteria and trying desperately to locate the protective barrier of her self-control, which seemed to have deserted her for the moment.

'I need someone here for a short time, till I've got myself together again,' she pleaded, hating the sense of panic that had turned her into a pathetic wimp. 'I don't know what's happening to me, Dante. I'm sorry to be a nuisance and I hate feeling so feeble about this. But the truth is, I'm absolutely terrified of being alone and falling asleep. Please. I am begging you. Stay for a while!'

The tip of his tongue moistened his lips as he contemplated her doubtfully.

'If this is a ploy—'

'It's not! I swear!' she half sobbed.

'You must talk to an expert—'

'I'm not mad!' she protested.

'No, but you're disturbed. You need to discover what has caused this,' he gritted. 'I've never seen you like this before. Something happened which is festering in your subconscious. You need to know what you did. Only then will you be able to deal with it.'

There was a long pause while she gazed at him anxiously, willing him to remain with her. Holding his warm, dry hand, she felt his strength flow into her. Dizzily she conceded that she needed him badly. Longed to feel his arms around her again, protective and comforting.

'Stay!' she croaked, full of longing for him.

He gave a small and resigned sigh. 'Very well. Just till you fall asleep,' he muttered grudgingly.

Virtually snatching his hand from hers, he sat down on the bed, plumping up the pillows behind him and settling down so that his back was turned to her.

In relief, Miranda snuggled as close as she dared. 'I wish I could understand why I have these dreams,' she mumbled.

He grunted. 'I should have thought that was obvious. When did they begin?'

'The night after you left.'

An icy silence stretched long into the semi-darkness. 'As I expected. I think you'd better go to sleep,' he growled.

But she wasn't ready to do so. Dante had found her that fateful night when she'd had that fever. Perhaps he could throw light on what had happened. He might have seen something that would explain what she'd done in her delirium—maybe an overturned table which might have caused her bruises, sheets which had wrapped themselves about her and made her think she was being restrained...

She had to know. A part of her life was missing and her brain was trying to fill in the gaps by giving her these awful nightmares. She'd ask him to discuss it. Now.

'Dante!'

Tentatively she touched his shoulder, the silk of his robe slipping beguilingly beneath her fingers. He flinched and she withdrew her hand. His body was hot, every muscle held in tension. He was hating this enforced togetherness. And she supposed that he was only staying with her to keep her quiet.

'Don't—do—that!' he gritted out.

She pressed her lips together in dismay. The days of curling up together like two spoons in a drawer were long gone. This was probably the last time he'd ever be physically close to her.

All because of someone who'd fed him lies—who?—and

her strange illness which had prompted her to fling champagne
about and thrash around in bed, thus sealing the death of her
marriage.

'That night—'

'I don't want to talk about it!'

She noticed that his fist had clenched so tightly that the
knuckles were white.

'I need to know what happened—!'

'Then talk to your boyfriend,' he said coldly. 'Or the people
in the clubs you frequented—'

'There was no boyfriend!' she declared vehemently, sitting
up and wriggling around to confront him. 'No clubs! No reason,' she added, her hair swinging around her angry face,
'other than an all-consuming fever that...'

Her voice tailed away. She gulped.

'An all-consuming fever,' he husked.

Anger had ceased to dominate his expression. His eyes had
fired with desire. His lips had parted over his teeth as his
breath hissed in and out in short, hot bursts. They were inches
away. In a moment, she imagined wistfully, she would be in
his embrace and the past would be forgotten.

She let her eyelids flutter down and waited, hoping for the
miracle to happen.

'*Hold me!*' she whispered, intending it to be a soundless
wish.

And yet he'd heard her, his impatient outbreath making her
snap open her eyes at once in alarm and disappointment.

'Damn you, Miranda! Stop using your body as a weapon!'
he snapped.

She blinked in confusion. 'What?'

He shook his head irritably. 'We have to live together in
harmony, Miranda! For the sake of that future relationship, I'll
give you the benefit of the doubt over the way you're behaving
at this moment. I am going to assume that you are *not* using
this as a cold-blooded opportunity to get me into bed. I'll be
charitable and believe that you're frightened and you're looking for comfort.'

Her face flamed with humiliation. Comfort and love. Wasn't everyone? she thought resentfully.

'Of course that's right!' she mumbled, appalled by her weakness for him.

He stood up, pulling his robe across his chest to cover it. Every gesture, the set of his body, told her that he was distancing himself from her emotionally. She bit her lip. He was going to leave. She'd handled this very badly.

'We can't allow ourselves to get into this kind of situation, Miranda,' he said harshly. 'I'm sorry that you're frightened and upset but there's a limit to what I can do for you. Or what I *want* to do.' His eyes burned into hers. 'You know perfectly well that if I hold you, we'll have sex because our bodies are still programmed to do so. I'm flesh and blood, as you know too well. You're a woman, in bed and provocatively dressed, and I haven't had sex for some time.'

'Sex,' she whispered. 'Is that all it is for you?'

'It's a powerful drug and we've become addicts,' he growled. 'But anything between us would be lust and nothing else and I'd be disgusted with myself afterwards. I'd also be angry with you. A sexual relationship would complicate our business arrangement. I'm sure you would agree.'

So cold. He might have been a total stranger. She began to withdraw into her shell, wrapping herself in her long-established defences so she would not be hurt again.

'Perhaps,' she suggested in compromise, hoping she sounded cool and composed, 'you could sit in the chair over there for a while.'

He studied her. She was conscious of her tumbling hair and the fact that the bedclothes no longer covered her. She had scrambled up with her body curled to one side, her nightdress settling in rich folds around her thighs and leaving her long legs bare.

His brooding stare lowered from her dishevelled hair and drowsy eyes to her throat, where a pulse beat hard and urgently. To her creamy shoulders. The curving line where her nightdress dipped and rose sinuously to hug her breasts.

Her defences crumbled in an instant. Flames licked through her body unmercifully.

'I think not,' he said thickly.

He raked a hand through his hair till it was uncharacteristically tousled. He looked almost vulnerable, his dark eyes huge and liquid. However hard she tried, she couldn't stop wanting him. And it was crucifying her.

There seemed to be a current flowing between them. A last remaining link perhaps, however tenuous, of the passions they had aroused in one another. He despised her—but he desired her, as well.

The evidence was all too obvious and she felt a spasm of excitement vibrating in every nerve of her body. Because there was one sure way to get rid of their unwanted lust. And before she realised what she was doing, she found herself saying recklessly,

'Dante…I can see that you hate being tied to me. I feel the same about you. I want to be back in control. Why don't we lay all the ghosts once and for all? We are married, after all—'

'Out of the question!' he exclaimed, knowing by her expression exactly what she had in mind.

To make love. To rid themselves of this need for one another. And to start again, cold, indifferent, businesslike.

Or would they?

She heaved in a breath, realising that they'd never know. He'd fight his desire all the way. But then it was easier for him. He'd never loved her as she'd loved him.

'I had thought you might be prepared to comfort me,' she faltered. 'Hold me securely until I slept.'

'And?' he challenged.

Trapped by his laser stare, she lowered her eyes, unable to understand why she couldn't get it into her head that he had never had any deep feelings for her. It seemed her heart just wouldn't accept that fact. Nor her body. It seemed inconceivable that she could ever contemplate sex without love. Worse, that she could want a man who had nothing but contempt for her.

And yet she seemed to be obsessed by Dante. He possessed her, body and soul, and she was alarmingly helpless in the face of her irrational passion. All her life she'd been in command of herself. Losing control like this was alarming. The situation had to change. She decided to be frank.

'I'm not going to beat about the bush. You said yourself that we want one another,' she defended quietly.

'And we must resist that, for our own self-respect,' he muttered.

Then she looked up at him, catching a wrench of despair crossing his face. Emboldened by the evidence of his dilemma, she spoke her mind.

'You say it's inevitable that these feelings will remain for a while—and you're right. What are we going to do when this happens again, then? Spend our spare time taking cold showers?'

'There can be no other solution,' he replied bleakly.

'You and I had sex without love for the whole of our marriage,' she pointed out with some tartness.

He might not have loved her, but he'd been perfectly willing to use her. She went cold. Had he found someone else?

Fury blazed in his eyes and his mouth compressed. 'That's no excuse to repeat it. I am not your comfort blanket!' he snarled. 'I will not be used to satisfy your needs! The situation is too delicate. I accept that this has been a difficult day for both of us but I am sure things will be easier in the morning. You're tough, Miranda. You'll get used to the lack of sex—'

'And you?' she asked unhappily.

One day he'd really fall in love. She felt her stomach cramp. Even if there wasn't anyone at the moment, there was a danger that he'd meet the love of his life one day. Another woman in his bed, as his wife. The pain racked her.

Another woman mothering Carlo. Then, Miranda thought in dismay, she'd really be defunct. Fear raced through her, draining what little strength she had. The danger had never dawned on her before. She wouldn't let that happen! But how could she ever prevent it?

'I can get used to anything if it means Carlo is happy,' Dante replied, his eyes like cold black pebbles. 'His welfare will always be uppermost in my mind. We have to make this work, Miranda! We can't let him down.'

She knew then that she would move heaven and earth to clear her name. Perhaps then, she thought wistfully, like many who were in arranged marriages, he'd eventually fall in love with her.

It was her only hope if she was to stay close to the two people who had captivated her heart.

'I know! I swear that I will do everything I can to make this a success!' she whispered, choked with emotion.

'Make sure you do.'

After one last look at her huge, bruised eyes, he spun around on his heel and strode rapidly into her sitting room. The light there flicked off, leaving her in the dark. The connecting doors closed softly and she heard the sound of a key turning.

A subdued Miranda slid beneath the bedclothes, her heart beating like a drum. As well as the nightmares when she went to bed, she'd be living one during each day. Being close to Dante and behaving with polite restraint would be harder than she could ever have believed. It would be torture to be in his company—and yet not able to reveal her true feelings.

He still held her heart in his hands. Despite everything, she loved him more than she could believe possible. Wanted him. As a friend, companion, a lover, a husband. Longed for his respect and admiration. And that all seemed a very long way from being realised.

'Oh, sweet heaven!' she whispered into the blackness of the room. 'Make me strong for Carlo's sake!'

Dante was wrong. It wouldn't be better in the morning. Miranda gritted her teeth, determined not to be destroyed by the situation. Tomorrow she might be calmer and able to deal with the problem.

Her life had been hard before and she had overcome it. Nothing was impossible. Not even winning Dante's approval and, one day, his love. Which meant she must become lovable in his eyes. A warm and inviting woman.

So she would have to change.

Dante had found her rigid self-control to be a barrier between them. But could she risk surrendering that and exposing herself to hurt?

Sleep would not come. After tossing and turning for a while, she gave up and slipped from the bed. By feeling her way across the room, she managed to locate the floor-to-ceiling window and the mechanism to pull back the drapes.

Immediately she felt soothed. Across the tar-black lake, village lights twinkled seductively and danced in the water with their shimmering gold reflections. The garden below was lit with soft-focus lamps, making it seem a magical place. A paradise in which Carlo could grow up.

Her heartbeat slowed. Yes. She could do it. It would take tenacity and grit, but she would slowly and surely establish her position as someone with high moral values and total devotion to the family. That was all that mattered.

Her thoughtful gaze fell on a figure, which had stepped out onto the terrace. Dante, dressed in jeans and a sweater, with the antenna of a baby alarm sticking out of his pocket. Miranda drew back a little, not wishing to be seen, but he didn't glance back at the house once.

Like her, he studied the view and she saw his high shoulders gradually ease to a more normal level. Head lowered, he began to pace up and down. For a while she watched in some sympathy, then she stumbled back to bed, somewhat consoled that he too had been disturbed, even though his agitation had probably only been caused by unrelieved lust.

And perhaps also, she thought wryly, by the idea of harbouring an alcoholic junkie under his roof!

For a long time she chewed over the situation. Gradually she came to the conclusion that, however ruthless he might be, he was also honest and fair. He'd acknowledged her distress and had realised that it had been a difficult day for her.

Hopefully their misunderstandings would be corrected. They must be, if she was to survive his suspicion.

One joy remained to boost her spirits. She smiled tenderly as she snuggled into the pillow. In the morning she would be with Carlo. And for that privilege, she would weather any storms and cope with any hardships.

She had a chance to prove herself. For the three of them to become a real family. And for that result, she would go to hell and back. And, she thought wryly, she probably would.

CHAPTER SEVEN

IT WAS A glorious morning. Some inner alarm woke her early and she hurried to take a shower and dress before Carlo woke. She wanted to be ready when he did.

Feeling very positive and excited and energised by the fabulous day, she pulled on the camisole and skirt of the suit she'd worn the day before, making mental plans to organise the packing of her clothes and effects in London. Her make-up was a hasty affair and she whisked her hair into a casual version of her usual neat chignon, the ends spiking out rather rakishly.

For half an hour she sat, drumming her fingers on the dressing table and making occasional adjustments to her make-up. And then she heard the key turn in the lock of the connecting door.

She leapt up, her heart in her mouth. Nervously she smoothed her skirt. Walked shakily to the door. And opened it.

Only Dante was in the room, dressed in a casual cream shirt and pale honey jeans, both so beautifully cut that they'd probably been made to measure. Miranda thought he could have just stepped off a designer catwalk.

He took one look at her pale, elated face. His mouth tightened and he turned.

'Carlo!' he called. 'Your surprise has arrived!'

Miranda heard a clatter as if a toothbrush had been dropped in a basin. She held her breath, hardly daring to believe that her son was really here. And then, there he was, tinier than she remembered, his hair longer, whiter, his small and much-adored face a picture of amazement.

'Mummy! Mummy!' he squealed and, laughing in delight, he ran barefooted to her, his arms outstretched in welcome.

'My darling!'

Swamped by emotion, she swept him up and hugged him close. Carlo's warm, plump arms wrapped around her neck and he squeezed so tightly that she almost choked.

'Oh, sweetheart!' she whispered, kissing his soft little cheek. 'Sweetheart!'

'Finish dressing him. He'll show you where we have breakfast.'

Her sparkling eyes flicked to Dante. He was walking out of the door and looking grim, his normally fluid body jerky and uncoordinated. Presumably with anger.

But she was too happy to care that he couldn't deal with Carlo's love for her. She was back with her son and life was improving by the minute.

'Why you cryin', Mummy?' Carlo demanded.

She beamed at him through a mist of tears.

'Laughing, not crying,' she told him softly. 'Sometimes when you laugh, it makes your eyes water. Shall we get you ready for breakfast? Show me where your things are.'

It was the beginning of a new life, she thought as Carlo slid from her arms and gleefully rushed to find his shoes and socks. She would risk everything to be accepted as Carlo's mother and Dante's wife.

She took a deep breath. She wanted their love. And would settle for nothing less.

But how? a little voice queried inside her. And she dismissed it because she could not find the answer.

'He seems very happy.'

She nodded in acknowledgement of Dante's comment and watched Carlo excitedly running into the *scuola materna*. She smiled. It was a lovely name for nursery school.

Carlo turned and waved, his rucksack bouncing on his back. They both waved back at him and grinned at his beam of pure delight before he grabbed a little friend's hand and ran into the nursery.

At first she'd been upset that Dante had told her Carlo must continue with his routine. She'd wanted to spend the whole day with her son and had fully expected Carlo to refuse when Dante had told him to get his rucksack for nursery.

But a beam had spread across Carlo's face as if the sun had come out and he'd raced off to collect the bag without a murmur. She'd been torn between disappointment for her own sake and relief that his life was continuing as normal.

'I thought he might not want to go this morning,' Dante mused, voicing Miranda's thoughts as their son disappeared through the double doors of the little school.

'He seemed a bit anxious the way he clung to me before breakfast,' she admitted.

'Yes.' Dante's voice grew sombre. 'I was worried that he might be unsettled for a while.'

'That's why I talked about getting my clothes and things sent here from England,' she explained. 'Then your suggestion about us all going off to Maggiore for tea and cakes after nursery seemed to set his mind at rest.'

'Blatant bribery, I'm afraid,' Dante said with a faint smile.

'It doesn't matter. Desperate needs, desperate measures!' She chuckled. 'The main thing is that he's convinced I'm here to stay.'

Dante looked at her thoughtfully. 'You are, aren't you?'

She met his wary eyes and wondered if he guessed how she felt when she did so. If he knew the bitter-sweet pangs of love that stabbed at her body over and over again.

'I will never leave,' she said quietly, not even attempting to conceal her adoration.

He jerked his head away, his expression tense. 'I wonder what they're having for lunch,' he said in an odd, over-bright tone. And he peered at a notice on the gate. 'Pasta and tomato sauce, boiled beef and green vegetables, fruit. Very good.'

The mood lightened, and Miranda laughed as they began to

walk away. 'Do they provide a menu every day?' she asked, impressed.

'Of course. Lunch is an important social occasion. It's virtually part of the curriculum.'

'Curriculum?' she repeated in amusement.

Dante grinned, and for her it was a huge breakthrough in their tricky relationship that he felt he could unbend a little towards her.

'*Daverro!* Indeed! Let me see. This term it's tastes and smells, opposites and colours. Nothing heavy. Just a general awareness of the differences in life. And they're emphasising friendship this week, too. Carlo is popular, they tell me,' he said with the touching pride of a doting father, 'because of his sunny nature. He loves being with other children—that's why he settled so well.'

'He's a very lovable child,' she said with affection. 'Open and outgoing.'

'Unlike you,' Dante muttered.

She winced. 'No problem with the language?' she asked, changing the subject hastily.

'A friendly smile goes a long way, it seems. And he's picking up more and more Italian phrases as the days go by.'

A friendly smile. Yes. It broke down barriers. It was something she could put into practice too.

'Children learn very quickly from their peers,' she said soberly.

'And need to be with them,' he agreed. 'I had my doubts about putting him in the school when Sonniva suggested it, but she was right. It took his mind off you and he was able to enjoy himself with children of his own age.'

'I'm glad he's settled so well,' she said softly. 'He'll have a good life here.'

Her eyes shone. Carlo was happy. She glanced at Dante's face and saw how strained he looked. The urge to reach out and take his arm, to snuggle into him and cheer him up, was overwhelming. But she didn't do that kind of thing.

Or *hadn't*. Had that been the problem? He'd criticised her

for being an ice queen with a harlot's heart. Told her that he never knew what she was thinking until they were in bed and making love—and even then he'd always wondered if it had been pure bodily gratification on her part.

Her shocked protests had washed over him. He claimed he didn't know her and, while her reticence had impressed him when she was his secretary, he hadn't expected it to continue when they were married.

But all her life she'd hidden her feelings—and the cause of them. It had been the only way to survive the hurt when she was eleven and her beloved father had disappeared for ever. And it had stood her in good stead when her mother had screamed at her that it was her fault because having kids meant you couldn't go out at the drop of a hat with your husband.

Miranda had also hidden the resentment she'd secretly felt within days of her father's disappearance, when she'd become the prime carer for her little sister so that her mother could have some kind of a life. Miranda thought of the invitations out to parties she had refused and, later, the dates she had turned down. It had been hard, staying at home and watching her mother getting ready to go out on the town instead.

Worse, it had been difficult to cope with the fact that Lizzie had always been the favourite. Miranda had never been loved like the ebullient Lizzie, or allowed the same freedom.

But she knew that resenting your mother and sister, or feeling angry and sorry for yourself, was wrong. Consequently she had told no one of this, determined not to play the victim. And so she had learnt to remain composed and silent, despite the volcanic emotions simmering within her.

Desperate needs…desperate measures. Why not, for once, behave as she wished—as she really felt? In the secret depths of her heart she was spontaneous and loving. Maybe she should abandon the habit of a lifetime and wear that heart on her sleeve. Wryly she looked at her arm. Looked then at Dante's.

On an impulse, she slid her arm through his and smiled up at him, her breath high in her throat as she waited nervously for his rejection. Instead, he gave her a tight little smile in return and lifted his eyebrow in a query.

'I wanted to thank you,' she said in barely concealed delight.

'For providing you with a luxury lifestyle?' he asked cynically.

Taking a deep breath and determined not to be rattled, she persevered.

'No. For being so kind to Lizzie. I managed to speak to her before she left. She was thrilled with your suggestion that you could lend her your car and Luca, to enable her to shop in Milan at your expense.' Her eyes danced. 'It was very clever of you, too. I don't think she even noticed that you'd got her on the evening flight, even though she'd been angling to stay for a week!'

For that, she had a genuine smile from him, Dante's eyes softening into what seemed like melted chocolate. Her heart beat faster and her pulse rate increased.

'Carlo told me he was going to paint you a picture today,' Dante murmured.

'Oh, really?' She beamed in delight. 'I can't wait!'

'You mean that!' He stared at her in surprise.

'Of course I do.' She fixed him with an earnest stare, her eyes huge with love for them both. 'Use your eyes, Dante. Trust your intuition. Would he love me so deeply if I hadn't loved him? If every small detail of his life wasn't of the utmost importance to me? I'm thrilled at the thought of having one of his pictures.' She smiled, encouraged by the softening of Dante's expression. 'I hope I can recognise what it is, though!'

To her delight, he gave a warm laugh. 'After holding his first painting and saying it was a lovely apple—then being told it was a train and it was upside down—I'm very wary of making any detailed comment!'

She giggled, a little wistful that she hadn't been there to see Carlo's first picture from nursery school. It was a silly little thing, but to her it was a huge step in her son's life, like that first word, the first step, and the first pair of shoes.

But Dante had missed those particular moments in his frantic travelling and she couldn't begrudge him this one. She knew now that he loved Carlo as much as she did.

Their son was the vital link between them—and could, perhaps, bring them together. Whenever either of them talked about him, it was with besotted smiles on their faces. She felt sure that Dante was beginning to realise the part she played in Carlo's happiness. More importantly, Dante must see now that she loved her child deeply. Maybe soon he'd question the rumours he'd heard about her.

She took a deep breath. Her marriage was worth saving. She'd fight for it with all her might.

Her spirits rose, and as she looked about her with more confidence, she realised they weren't retracing their steps to the *palazzo*. Earlier, they had walked with Carlo to the nursery along the improbably named Salita Cappuccini, climbing steep cobbled steps to the top of the hill. Now they were heading down an equally steep set of cobbled steps lined with small boutiques.

'I'm intrigued. Is this a silent mystery tour?' she asked with a laugh.

Dante looked a little sheepish. 'Sorry. I was thinking about something. I was miles away. No, it occurred to me that until we can get your clothes from England, you'll need one or two things to tide you over. I thought you'd like to do a bit of shopping. And perhaps get your bearings in Bellagio town itself.'

'That's very thoughtful!' she exclaimed gratefully. 'I was wondering how I could make these clothes last before I was thrown out of Italy for vagrancy.'

His grin flashed and she felt as if she'd drunk heady wine.

'You would never look a mess,' he assured her drily.

And then he was greeting acquaintances as they made their way down the hill, drawing her closer as he did so.

Instead of making her happier, this set alarm bells ringing. It dawned on her that his apparent friendliness could be just part of his request that they should keep up appearances. Her joy died.

'You'll need some casual clothes and a bathing costume. Perhaps something for the evening,' he told her. 'And this is just the place to buy everything.'

Not even noticing how subdued she'd become, he swept her into an elegant boutique and settled himself in an armchair, leaving her to the attentions of a beautiful young female assistant.

Miranda went through the mechanics of choosing stopgap clothes and shoes without much enthusiasm and then began to try on some demure one-piece swimsuits.

She heard him laugh long and hard in a way she hadn't heard for a long time. Through a gap in the curtain she could see Dante still chuckling over something the young woman had said. The assistant was leaning over him—probably swamping him with perfume, Miranda thought waspishly— and offering him a cappuccino.

Feeling sick with jealousy, she glared at herself in the boring swimsuit. She ought to be bolder. More risqué. Every instinct told her to fight for her man with fair means or foul.

And before she could get cold feet, she grabbed a cotton robe from a hook and tied it around herself. Unnoticed by Dante, who was now surrounded by enthusiastically chattering female assistants, she padded over to the rack of bikinis and grimly selected a turquoise one to take back to the booth.

When she tried it on, she saw that it looked fabulous. Her stomach was very flat but her breasts and hips still held their womanly curves. If he saw this…

No. She dared not. Such behaviour was too outrageous. And yet… This was for her marriage. Desperate measures… For the family she loved.

Taking a deep breath to quell her nerves, she pulled back a tiny part of the curtain so that only her head poked around it.

'Darling!' she called as seductively as she dared. The encircling women looked around and he stood up, surprise etched in every line of his face. 'I'm not sure about this,' she said with an apologetic smile. 'I'd like your opinion.'

'My pleasure. *Permesso*,' he murmured to the women and found a way through them.

Miranda drew back into the confines of the deep changing booth, trying to look utterly natural even though she was shaking like a leaf.

Dante's hand eased back the curtain enough to allow him in. And then he seemed to freeze. The curtain swung back into place. His eyes raked her hungrily.

'What do you think?' she asked in a throaty kind of voice. And she lost her nerve. 'Or perhaps this one would be better…'

Bending down in confusion, she picked up the one-piece, becoming awkwardly aware that her breasts had fallen forwards invitingly and that her loosened hair now tumbled luxuriously about her pink face.

'Both,' he said hoarsely. 'One for public, one for…'

His reaction was so startling that she took a risk she would never have dreamed of taking if her marriage and her child were not threatened.

Stepping closer so they were almost touching, so that the fire in his body heated her skin even from an inch or two away, she lifted her head and finished the sentence for him.

'One for you and you alone?' she whispered daringly, with soft longing.

He gave an inarticulate mutter. His hands caught her slender waist and he pulled her into him. Their mouths met in a sweet, exploring kiss, which became harder, harsher, more urgent.

In a delirium, she held his face between her palms, adoring the smoothness of his skin, the wonderful pleasure of his lips on hers, the smell of him, the fresh taste of his mouth, the skill of his kisses as he slowly drove her back against the wall.

His hand was cupping her breast and she groaned because it had been so long since he'd done that. The feel of his fingers as they teased her nipple into a fiercely thrusting peak was driving her mad. And then his head dipped and she felt the warm wetness of his mouth there.

Through half-opened eyes she saw him suckling at her breast and her breath caught in a spasm of love as she looked down at his enraptured face. His eyes were closed, the silky fringe of black lashes a dark crescent on his cheekbones.

'Oh, Dante!' she breathed.

He stiffened and detached himself. When he gazed down at her languorous face, there was nothing in his expression to reveal how he felt—except for the burning of his dark eyes.

'I'll be outside,' he said thickly. And left before she could reply.

She reached out to the chair in the booth and all but fell onto it, her legs quite weak. Her reflection startled her. She looked as if she'd been ravished and had enjoyed every minute.

Starry-eyed, she hastily dressed, convinced now that they would make love quite soon. And that a closeness would slowly develop between them. He couldn't keep his hands off her! she exulted.

'They're delivering the things I bought,' she announced breathlessly to him when she joined his brooding figure outside the shop. 'I had some funny looks from the assistants, though,' she added, her face pink with embarrassment.

'Good. It was a clever idea of yours,' he said quite casually.

She blinked. 'What was?'

'Hauling me into the changing booth,' he drawled. 'Word will get out that we're crazy about one another and that we take any opportunity to touch. Take my arm. Let's continue the deception, shall we, while I show you around Bellagio?'

Miranda tagged along the quaint, narrow streets beside him, her head whirling. Had he kissed her because he'd found her irresistible, or because he'd seen a chance to pretend they had a normal marriage? And how would she ever know? she thought with exasperation.

'The lake is shaped like an upside-down Y. Bellagio sits where the three arms of Lake Como meet,' Dante was telling her in jerky, polite tones as they sauntered down the street, their arms romantically entwined.

His head bent to hers attentively. If she didn't know better, she thought bitterly, she'd think they were similar to the many lovers she could see gazing into one another's eyes. Only Dante's travel-guide delivery made her think differently.

'It's generally accepted to be one of the loveliest spots in Italy,' he continued.

An elderly couple smiled fondly at them, clearly imagining Dante to be whispering sweet nothings instead of spouting the contents of a brochure.

'Really?' she said but he didn't appear to notice her sadness.

'*Certo,*' he assured her in a low growl. He was hating this, she thought. Loathing their closeness. 'As you can see, it is unspoiled and picturesque, despite the visitors who flock here.'

They walked along an arcaded *piazza* and while he was murmuring textbook details about Roman cohorts coming to Como for rest and recuperation two thousand years ago she was trying to distance herself from her reaction to his inherently seductive voice and gestures so that she could think of a way to discover his true feelings about her.

If he hated her, she could work on that by proving her innocence—somehow. Given time she could turn lust into love, perhaps. But if he was truly indifferent...

'Nero came here. Da Vinci, Verdi, Rossini, Liszt, Wordsworth, Shelley... They found it inspired creativity—'

'OK. That's enough. You've sold it to me,' she said, uncomfortable with his detachment.

'What?'

'I can read the guide books later,' she muttered.

'We're here to be seen and for people to notice us and comment on our manner together,' he told her tightly. 'It would look odd if we walked in icy silence.'

'We could talk about things that matter to us,' she suggested quietly.

'And risk a row? It would be preferable to thrash out our differences in private. Ah,' he said, sounding relieved to have the chance of a diversion. 'Here's where the ferryboats leave. Something you need to know. I do have a private motor launch moored below the *palazzo*,' he told her, 'but Carlo loves the public boats because they serve drinks and food. In any case, you'd need the car ferry—which leaves further up there—' he waved a vague hand to their left '—if you want to explore the opposite shores comprehensively.'

Private. Public. Yes, she thought in sudden inspiration. She would get Dante into a private situation and see how he responded to her when nobody was around as a witness.

Cheered, she considered his last remark. 'I don't have a car,' she pointed out.

'Not yet. As my wife and Carlo's mother, you can have anything you want, remember? It's one of the prices I am prepared to pay. I give, you take.'

She only lacked one thing she desired. Dante's love.

'A small car would be great,' she said cautiously. 'But I don't like being beholden to you for money. That's why I wanted to work and be independent.'

'Then I will give you an allowance and you can spend it as you wish.' To her surprise he bent closer, his mouth nuzzling her ear. 'Cars, jewellery, dresses, sexy underwear…'

She quivered, rivulets of heat flowing through her at the husky suggestion in his voice. 'You'd like me to buy—!' she began with a breathless hope, and then he broke away.

'Felipe! Maria!' he exclaimed, warmly triple-kissing a dark-haired woman and hugging her companion with affection. 'Allow me to present my wife, Miranda. Darling, these are my good friends Felipe and Maria, who looked after my uncle's *palazzo* when he was away.'

With a sinking heart, she summoned up a smile. Dante must have seen them coming. That was why he'd murmured something seductive to get a suitable reaction from her.

His friends would have seen the blush that had crept up her face, the lift of her head as she'd gazed adoringly into Dante's eyes… Oh, how could she have been so stupid?

'How do you do—?' she began politely, swallowing her disappointment.

'*Piacere, Contessa!*'

Felipe bowed low and air-kissed her hand. But his eyes twinkled back at her and she decided she liked him enough to make her own smile genuine.

'Welcome,' enthused Maria, kissing her several times. 'You are as beautiful as Dante claimed. No wonder he was lost without you! He was a different person when he knew you were well enough to return.'

'Was he?'

Miranda's heart stopped for a brief moment before resuming a louder, faster beat. She longed for that to be true.

'To begin with, when we met, we thought he was naturally grumpy,' confided Felipe with a grin. 'But, ah, when he knew you were on your way here the sun came out and he began to sing in the garden—'

'Don't give all my secrets away!' joked Dante. But he looked uncomfortable.

Miranda was intrigued by what the couple had said. Surely Dante's marked change of mood couldn't be explained *purely* by a relief that Carlo would be more settled? Or was she trying to fool herself?

'…meet for dinner,' Maria was saying. 'But we are late for the Rapido to Como. Excuse us. We will talk more later, yes?'

After a welter of kisses and farewells, they hurried off.

'Did you sing?' she asked at once.

He shrugged and seemed shifty. 'I might have done. Often I'll have the refrain of a tune in my head and I sing when I'm alone.'

'You weren't alone,' she pointed out. 'Felipe heard you.'

'He might have done,' he conceded. 'You must understand, though, that in accordance with Italian custom, Felipe exaggerates,' Dante added shortly. 'He was being gallant. Telling you what you want to hear.'

'Is that what you do, Dante? What you've done throughout our marriage?' she asked tensely.

'No. I have lived so long in England that I've lost the art of effusive flattery. I say what I mean, though perhaps not quite so bluntly as the English.'

She thought about this. 'Felipe genuinely seemed to think you were pleased because I was on my way here,' she persisted, hoping to get to the truth.

'I'm sure he and Maria were subjected to conversations with my mother, in which she enthused over my feelings for you,' he drawled. 'He would have assumed that was why I appeared to be happy—whereas we know different.'

'Your mother certainly seems convinced of your adoration,' Miranda mused, breathing hard and fast. Sonniva, she mused, was a perceptive woman, shrewd and honest…

'Some people have rose-tinted vision,' he dismissed. 'They see what they want to see. Like Felipe and Maria. But…they have been good friends to me since I arrived,' he added and she had the distinct impression that he was keen to avoid further discussion. 'They live in the villa not far from us,' he explained. 'We'll see a lot of them, as they have a boy of Carlo's age.'

'Good. I like them,' Miranda said demurely. For the moment she'd let Dante off the hook. But all her instincts told her that he was hiding something from her. She hoped it was his true feelings. 'I look forward to meeting them again. I'm sure we could all be good friends.'

'You seem to be accepting the fact that you'll live here in future. No regrets, I assume?' he asked, his expression tense.

'None. I'll be with Carlo, won't I?' *And you,* she left unsaid.

'You'll enjoy the lifestyle, of course,' he observed, a cynical tone to his voice.

'You're thinking I'm looking forward to being the wife of a wealthy man and sweeping from one grand palace to another. But that wouldn't be enough for me,' she said, determined to put him straight about her potential as a gold-digger.

'You want more?'

'Not in the way you think.'

He shot her a look. 'I don't understand.'

'No. You thought I married you for material gain,' she said with sadness. How could he ever have believed that? 'Dante. Was I ever extravagant? Did you see any signs of greed in me?'

He frowned, as well he might. 'No,' he admitted.

'Did I know you were well off when I worked for you?'

'You could see I had a good lifestyle,' he grunted.

'But not flamboyant. You went everywhere by taxi as many people do in London. Your apartment in the City was not in a fashionable area although it was spacious and expensively furnished. You dressed well, but...' She smiled. 'You're Italian. It's part of your culture. If I'd been hunting for a rich man, I'd have gone for Guido.' She frowned, a bad taste in her mouth. Then dismissed it because her argument was so important. 'He flung his money around as if he had bottomless pockets. He has a Maserati. Eats only in the best celebrity restaurants. Wears a lot of jewellery. Everyone in the office thought he was loaded. Why, then, if I'd been truly mercenary, would I have set my sights on you?'

'I don't know. I am at a loss,' he said slowly.

She leaned into him a little. 'Listen,' she said softly. 'Since I was very young, my only wish has been to spend my life with someone I love. Do you believe *that*?'

'I think you do care for Carlo, yes,' he said, looking guarded.

She beamed. It wasn't quite what she'd meant, but nevertheless it was a milestone. 'And you accept that he wasn't starved of love?'

Dante looked uncomfortable. 'Perhaps my informant made a mistake.'

'Call the nanny and find out,' she urged. 'I have her new number. She'll complain that she wasn't allowed enough time with Carlo!'

'I have seen enough. I don't need to. I apologise for doubting your maternal instincts,' he said stiffly.

'And for doubting my love for you?' she asked, her heart beating hard.

His head jerked away, his profile suddenly stern. 'I can't pretend that your infidelity never happened,' he clipped and she realised she had a long way to go before she proved her innocence to him. 'The next week or so will be difficult for both of us. But we'll settle into some kind of working arrangement, providing you like it enough here.'

'Like it?' she cried, hope lifting the burden she'd carried from her shoulders. 'How could I not? It's a bonus that Bellagio is so beautiful. I love the lake and the mountains and the romantic little villages. I like the friendliness of the people who smile and nod at us even though they don't know who we are. I like to see the affection youngsters and their parents show towards older relatives. I like your friends. In fact,' she added, glancing around her fondly, 'I like Italians very much.'

'I'm glad,' Dante said drily. 'You'd find life hard if you didn't.'

'Mmm. They're wonderfully…free with their emotions, aren't they?' she mused.

She had been watching them for a while. Everywhere she looked, it seemed that people were gesticulating as they conducted lively exchanges. They stood close to one another as if they had no idea of personal space. And yet already she'd noticed that what initially seemed like fiery arguments often ended with laughter and hugs.

She sighed wistfully because here and there she could see courting couples gazing in rapture at one another, content, it seemed, just to breathe the same air, to be on the same planet.

'You envy their lack of inhibition?' Dante asked quietly.

'Yes,' she admitted. 'I do.'

And she vowed to allow the Italian love of free expression to seep into her. It was what he'd been used to. No wonder he'd thought her cold and unresponsive.

'Me too.' Dante's brooding eyes studied his surroundings. 'You know, I was so intent on handling the London end of the business, marrying you and setting up home there, that I didn't realise how much I missed Italy until I came back here to live.'

She absorbed this without comment. But she was stunned. He hadn't been happy in England. She pursed her lips, contemplating the fact that he'd been in virtual exile from the country of his birth.

Scanning the bustling promenade, she compared the greyness of the city of London and the vibrant colours all around them; the roar of the capital city's traffic, the dirt and the smell of petrol fumes…and the partially traffic-free Bellagio, where stately ferries ploughed their way across a glittering lake. The hurried, preoccupied Londoners wrapped in their own concerns…and the lively Italians hell-bent on living life to the full and including any passing stranger who caught their attention.

'I understand why you want Carlo to live here,' she said soberly. 'I think it's perfect for him. You love your house and its setting and I've fallen in love with it too. Because of that, I'm sure we can all be happy together in time.'

He looked disbelieving. 'Happiness? Very unlikely,' he said with a cynical drawl.

'Wait and see.' She felt shaky, as if she were poised on the edge of a precipice. She had to make him believe their marriage could be more than a façade. 'We must both work to that end.'

There was a long pause. 'Too much has happened. Too much anger, too many scars that can never heal. But I'll settle for a harmonious relationship. I'm relieved you're falling in with my plans.'

'I'll do everything I can to let people believe we have a good marriage,' she said earnestly.

Imperceptibly she moved closer to him and they walked along almost hip to hip. She felt him give a little shudder and knew he felt a physical interest in her. First, she thought, they'd have sex. And then it would gradually turn to a trusting, loving relationship.

She was in seventh heaven. Although she was dazzled by the breathtaking views, charmed by Bellagio and overwhelmed by the pleasure of being close to Dante, she was nevertheless

OFFICIAL OPINION POLL

ANSWER 3 QUESTIONS AND WE'LL SEND YOU
4 FREE BOOKS AND A FREE GIFT!

0074823 |||||||||||| |||||||| |||||||

FREE GIFT CLAIM # 3953

YOUR OPINION COUNTS!

Please tick TRUE or FALSE below to express your opinion about the following statements:

Q1 Do you believe in "true love"?

"TRUE LOVE HAPPENS ONLY ONCE IN A LIFETIME."
○ TRUE
○ FALSE

Q2 Do you think marriage has any value in today's world?

"YOU CAN BE TOTALLY COMMITTED TO SOMEONE WITHOUT BEING MARRIED."
○ TRUE
○ FALSE

Q3 What kind of books do you enjoy?

"A GREAT NOVEL MUST HAVE A HAPPY ENDING."
○ TRUE
○ FALSE

YES, I have scratched the area below.

Please send me the 4 FREE BOOKS and FREE GIFT for which I qualify. I understand I am under no obligation to purchase any books, as explained on the back of this card.

4 FREE BOOKS AND A FREE GIFT

P4LI

Mrs/Miss/Ms/Mr _____ Initials _____

BLOCK CAPITALS PLEASE

Surname _____

Address _____

_____

Postcode _____

Visit us online at www.millsandboon.co.uk

The Reader Service™ — Here's how it works:

THE READER SERVICE™
FREE BOOK OFFER
FREEPOST CN81
CROYDON
CR9 3WZ

NO STAMP
NECESSARY
IF POSTED IN
THE U.K. OR N.I.

alert enough to realise that the set of his body had changed quite dramatically.

It was as though he had been holding himself back before, as if he, too, had imposed some kind of restraint on himself.

When he pointed out the villages across the lake, he became more animated and flamboyantly Italian. Responding to an inner urge, she put her arm around his waist. When he stiffened, she thought he'd shrug it off. But his muscles relaxed again and he slid his arm around her slender waist, making her heart sing with joy.

As they wandered along, she noticed that they were attracting admiring glances. People smiled at them fondly. One day, she promised herself, this would be for real.

Feeling light-headed, she listened with pleasure to Dante's enthusiastic descriptions of the sumptuous gardens in the villas open to the public.

'You really love Bellagio, don't you?' she laughed, almost drunk with happiness, when he paused for breath.

He scowled and cleared his throat. 'Everything about it. There's so much to show you. The day after tomorrow we'll take a drive inland...'

He had paused. Like her, he had seen that all eyes seemed to be elsewhere, a murmur of voices buzzing excitedly about something. She looked back over her shoulder and discovered the focus of everyone's attention.

'Oh, look, Dante! A bride and groom!' she exclaimed softly. The bride looked very young, perhaps as old as she'd been when she'd married Dante. Her dress was the purest white and the white roses in her dark, glossy hair gave her a touching fragility. 'Isn't she lovely?' Miranda breathed dreamily.

'Beautiful,' he agreed, his voice sombre.

She frowned, puzzled. 'Where's everyone else? The bridesmaids, guests... There's just the couple and a photographer!'

'It's the custom. They're being photographed in romantic settings.'

He sounded choked. Emotion had claimed her too. The

bride looked as if she might burst with love. The fresh-faced groom couldn't take his eyes off his adoring wife.

That was how it had been for her, Miranda thought, a pain wrenching at her heart. But not for Dante.

With everyone watching fondly, the couple posed at the foot of the cobbled steps then beneath the arcade. She and Dante looked on, each with their own thoughts, as the photographer persuaded the couple into an artistic pose by a stone balustrade, with the lake and mountains in the background.

So loving, she thought as they laughed and giggled their way to the gangplank of the passenger ferry for another shot.

Somehow Dante's hand had crept into hers. It was poignant, watching the couple. They hadn't a care in the world. They were starting married life and were confident it would be roses all the way. She felt tears welling up and fought hard to suppress them as she contemplated the ruins of her own marriage.

'*Complimenti*,' Dante murmured as the rapturous lovebirds wandered past them on their way to another venue.

The bride gave him a sweet smile, which became even warmer when she met Miranda's wistful eyes. Her new husband said something in Italian and Dante's grip tightened as the couple moved on.

'What did he say?' she asked, where once she would have kept silent.

Dante didn't look at her, but watched the bride and groom running like children to a seat by a large floral display.

'He returned the compliment,' he said eventually. 'He said he imagined we were recalling our own wedding.'

'I was,' she admitted shakily.

She remembered with a sigh that she had been in a dream the whole day. Dante's lovemaking that night had been tender and profoundly passionate.

She also remembered how his face had glowed with an inner radiance. Her heart thudded. Could Guido have been wrong? Had Dante loved her when they got married? She'd truly believed that he did at the time.

Though, she thought with a shiver, his rapturous expression

on their wedding day could have been due to something else: imagining himself stepping into Amadeo's shoes and inheriting a fortune.

'Lunch,' he muttered, drawing her to a table overlooking the lake. He seemed preoccupied and thoughtful.

Daringly she blurted out, 'I wish it was like it used to be between us.'

He winced as though he felt the same pain that shafted through her body.

'Those days of innocence are gone,' he growled.

And with that harsh put-down, he picked up the menu and annoyingly disappeared behind it.

But she persevered, risking an outright snub. It was a chance she had to take.

'You can't deny that it would be wonderful if we could be *truly* together,' she ventured. 'Easier all round. No pretences,' she added haltingly.

He lowered the menu sufficiently for her to see his dark, intense eyes.

'Yes,' he rasped and dashed her hopes by following that with, 'but we have to accept that it would be impossible under the circumstances.'

'Nothing's impossible—' she choked out.

'I think there is something you should understand about Italian men, Miranda,' he said tightly. 'Honour is very important to them.'

His mouth twisted but he kept his head down, his eyes lowered to the damask tablecloth. And in a bleak voice he continued, 'The worst insult you could imagine would be to call a man *cornuto*. Do you know what that means?'

Glumly she shook her head. But she could guess.

'It's a cuckold,' he said. 'A man who's wife has been unfaithful.' His eyes lifted to hers—hot, burning, indicating the seething emotions he was repressing. 'It pains me that anyone could call me a cuckold—and the fact that if they did I would have to stay silent, because it's true. I try to forget it, to put it aside, but it rips me apart to think of you with other men.

When I look at you I think of their hands roaming over your body and I can barely contain my anger and shame!'

Hot tears threatened and she beat them back furiously.

'I did not betray you,' she insisted. 'I have always been faithful.' Taking a deep breath, she decided to seize the moment and added in a low whisper, 'I have always loved you.'

And she waited for his response, her heart in her mouth. Everything depended on this. Her future happiness, Carlo's. Please make him believe me, she thought, her hands tightening into fists beneath the table.

'A commendable try,' he drawled, his skin taut with disapproval over the contours of his face as he pretended to scan the menu. 'But I know the truth. Understand this, Miranda. I can *never* forgive you.' His eyes lifted to hers and in them she saw her own bleak misery.

She felt that he'd thrust a knife into her heart. Her confession of love, her attempts to penetrate his barrier of hatred and mistrust, had been in vain. He'd made up his mind. They'd be polite strangers for years to come.

She sat silent and stunned and deeply hurt by his intransigence as Dante beckoned for service.

Conscious of the waiter prompting her, she mechanically put in her order, knowing she wouldn't be able to do more than toy with her food.

Then, averting her head in misery, she pretended to be fascinated by the boats crossing the lake, but all she could see were white blurs in a mist of blue because tears had sprung into her eyes and were clogging up her throat.

It seemed she was no nearer to saving her marriage. Maybe, she thought in a flood of despair, there was no hope, after all.

CHAPTER EIGHT

SHE felt battered and bruised. If it hadn't been for Carlo, she would have gone back to the *palazzo* and wept in her room till she could weep no more. Then she would have taken the next flight home, to prepare for a lonely and loveless future.

But of course she had to stick this out. And she knew that in two hours they were to collect him for his treat in Maggiore. She had no intention of appearing red-eyed and defeated in front of her son.

Because of that she conquered her urge to sob her heart out and forced herself to reply to Dante's inconsequential remarks during the meal.

'Yes, thank you,' she said politely. 'The *strangozzi* is excellent.'

Resolutely avoiding his eyes, she jabbed her fork into the noodles and scooped up some of the anchovy and peppers with it.

'More wine?' he enquired solicitously. 'And please smile occasionally.'

Repressing the urge to say 'what for?' she managed a strained smile and a nod. As he filled her glass, she muttered,

'You care very much what people think of us, don't you?'

He leaned forward as if he were saying something intimate and romantic.

'You know perfectly well that I don't want Carlo to become aware that anything's amiss. And that means other people must be convinced of our unity.'

She heaved a huge sigh. That was all he cared about. Well, she wasn't going to continue this farce. Dante had to be forced to accept her innocence.

'I want to talk to you later,' she muttered. 'When he's in bed.'

'Look at me.'

Her eyes lifted in sullen query. 'Well? I'm looking.'

'You can't sulk. Lovers gaze into one another's eyes,' he said huskily.

She winced. 'We're married,' she retorted, trying to hide her anguish.

Dante reached across the table and caught her hand in his. While she rejoiced in the warmth of his grip, she had to steel herself against the urge to leap up and run away from the cruel charade they were playing.

'It was part of our agreement that you would keep up appearances,' he reminded her with soft menace. 'You agreed to this. And confirmed it only moments ago.' His voice grew husky. 'You will look at me as if you love me. As if I am the only man in the world for you.'

His fingers began to stroke her palm and she could bear it no longer.

'Please, Dante! I want to leave!' she whispered in desperation.

A moment's pause. Then, 'Yes. Why not?'

And to her surprise, he flung some notes on the table and drew her to her feet, calling back something to the waiter, who had come running to see what was the matter.

Dante held her hard against him as they walked away. They turned into a narrow side-street and suddenly the noise and bustle became a distant murmur. She was lost in her own misery and had never felt more alone. Pretending they were happily married was harder than she'd ever imagined. And they had months and years of it to come! She ground her teeth.

'I'm surprised you didn't refuse my request,' she muttered tetchily.

Dante's breath sounded harsh. 'It wouldn't surprise anyone to imagine that we're hurrying off to spend the rest of the day in bed.'

Miranda stiffened and froze. '*What?*' she choked in horror. 'You told a waiter—?'

'No!' he said impatiently. 'I wouldn't dream of doing anything so crass. But he is a man and knows of the whirlwind of passion that can strike at any time and he will put two and two together—'

'And it matters what a waiter thinks?' she snapped, stalking on again.

She felt suffocated. Her life wasn't her own. It was composed of lies and deception.

'Yes. Because he'll gossip,' Dante answered tersely. 'My arrival in the town has been noted with interest. Yours has been eagerly awaited. Haven't you noticed everyone staring?'

She was used to that. People always stared when she walked about with Dante—though he'd always asserted they'd been looking at *her*.

'I suppose you're delighted with your morning's work,' she grouched, barely able to hold back her temper. 'The whole of Bellagio will soon know how *perfect* our marriage is! It's hateful, having to pretend! I feel I'm deceiving everyone. Your mother, your friends…'

She clenched her teeth to stop a sob from escaping. Oh, Carlo, she thought, if only you knew what I have to do to be with you!

Dante turned her to face him, his eyes glittering with a frightening intensity.

'What makes you think you have the monopoly on feelings?' he said tautly. 'Why do you imagine you're the only one who is finding this an utter nightmare? That I don't loathe the deception too? This situation is a million miles from what I really want. But it's all I'm going to get so I have to put up with it.'

Her mouth clammed shut. His misery affected her strangely. She wanted to make him happy, to see him content. But that would never be, not while they were trapped in this farcical marriage.

'Oh, hell!' he groaned. 'That's all I need, right at this minute!'

He was glowering darkly at a villa decorated with blue and white streamers and matching rosettes. Bows had been tied in blue and white ribbons on every railing spike of the surrounding fence and banners had been strung across the lane.

She frowned. 'What is it?'

'*This* is where the groom lives,' he muttered, storming ahead. Only to be confronted with another villa similarly decorated, this time in pink and white. Dante stopped and glared at the offending gaiety. 'I could do without having weddings thrust down my throat!' he growled.

In a flash of intuition she jerked out, 'You wish you had true love, too.'

He winced at the joyful ribbons fluttering in the breeze and looked away.

'Don't we all?'

It was her turn to wince. As they walked back to the *palazzo* in total silence, she felt sadness creep through her, filling every part of her yearning body. He felt trapped. He was young and virile and facing the daunting prospect of marriage to a woman he didn't love—for the foreseeable future.

She shrank at the thought. Maybe they had both made a mistake in thinking that they must stay together for Carlo's sake. For Dante, a civilised divorce and shared custody might be a better solution.

Though she would need assurances about her future role if she was ever to agree to such a drastic step. And she didn't know how she would cope when he remarried—as he surely would.

Miranda stomped along miserably, trying to sort out the mess they'd made of their lives. She knew one thing. Whatever they decided, she must clear the air. She couldn't let him think she was a bad mother and an unfaithful wife. He had to know that she hadn't treated her marriage vows lightly, even if *he* had.

And that, she mused optimistically, might change his attitude towards her. She brightened up a little.

'I think we need some time apart now. This has been tougher than I imagined,' Dante muttered as he unlocked a small gate into the garden and deactivated the alarm. He glared at her. 'When we collect Carlo later, I expect you to make an effort to be friendly towards me.'

'Oh, I will,' she assured him. 'I'll give it my all. And tonight,' she added with steely determination, 'we will talk this situation through. There's some things we must get straight. And we need some ground rules.'

'We'll need more than rules to keep us in check,' he growled, and before she could ask him to explain the cryptic statement he strode away rapidly through an archway of lemon trees.

She filled the time wandering in the garden, trying to come to terms with Dante's feelings about her. Tonight she would make him reveal who'd told him all those lies about her. And they'd confront this person together, she vowed grimly, demanding evidence.

And somehow they'd discover what had happened that night she was taken ill. Maybe a friend had come round before the flu had hit her—though she didn't know anyone who'd be able to knock back so much champagne.

Her eyes darkened as she gazed out over the untroubled lake. The overwhelming temptation was to retreat into her shell and pretend that nothing hurt her. But now she realised that hiding her feelings had led Dante to believe she didn't love him. Or Carlo.

She had to go for broke. Dante needed to know how deep her feelings were, even if that meant risking his contempt and rejection.

It was an unnerving prospect. Nothing she had done so far—concealing her misery at her father's death, shouldering her sister's upbringing and suppressing her longing for fun and freedom—had been as hard as this.

But she loved Carlo and she loved Dante with all her heart. Misguided though it might be, she harboured a fancy in the back of her mind that if she persevered they could be a real family again. It was worth the try, worth the risk of being hurt.

Nervous but resolved, she checked her watch and saw to her surprise that it was time to collect Carlo.

At first, she and Dante were a little strained and false when they met him at the nursery. Their chatter was ridiculously bright and bordering on the inane. But soon she was caught up in her love for her child and the fun of seeing the world through his eyes.

'Dat's Mummy,' he said proudly, presenting her with a painting consisting entirely of muddied splodges. 'Mummy on de floor.'

'It's lovely!' she enthused, spotting a small smear of blue—presumably her—in the middle of the brown swirls. 'What am I doing on the floor?'

'Larfing,' Carlo said with a giggle and she swept him into her arms. 'Mummy larfs lots,' he told his father. 'Mummy loves me lots. I love Mummy.'

And she was subjected to an affectionate stranglehold. The ice had been broken and Carlo had confirmed the fact that she adored him.

From that moment on, gradually Dante and she grew more natural and spontaneous in their reactions and the atmosphere between them eased.

And their togetherness had a sweet poignancy that was not lost on her. Dante—at the moment—was *playing* at happy families. She was doing it for real.

By the evening, her emotions were in a tangle. She had loved every minute of her time with Dante and her beloved son. And wished it could be like this all the time because in this make-believe world there were no nightmares, no accusations of infidelity and no lack of love.

Instead, there was fun, laughter and affection. And lovely silly games, she thought in amusement as Dante plotted to 'chase Mummy' with Carlo, and began to stalk towards her menacingly.

'No, help! Help!' she squealed.

She had let her hair down, literally, and her white-blonde mane streamed out behind her as she dashed barefooted through the hall with Dante and a delighted Carlo in hot pursuit.

Pretending to trip over her flowing silk skirt, she allowed herself to be caught and they all collapsed in a laughing heap on the soft Persian rug.

Carlo flung his arms around her neck in his trademark stranglehold. 'I 'ove you, Mummy.'

'I love you too, sweetheart,' she said tenderly, giving him a kiss.

'Mummy's pretty,' he said proudly, pulling experimentally at her soft coral top and accidentally revealing the lace of her strapless bra. He looked to his father for confirmation.

'Yes,' he agreed in a low tone, though she didn't dare look at him. His voice was seductive enough. 'Very pretty.'

'Kiss Daddy!' Carlo demanded.

She hesitated, her eyes flicking to Dante's where he lay winded beside her. This was a bridge too far. Hastily she busied herself with sliding her narrow shoulder straps into place and wriggling the top back down to cover the soft skin of her exposed midriff.

'Kiss Daddy!' Carlo repeated, his face puckering anxiously.

She managed to smile in reassurance. Dante was beautifully smooth-shaven, she thought, her heart jerking with love. And devastatingly handsome, particularly now that his bow-tie had come undone in the mêlée and his top button was undone. That, the glimpse of tanned throat and his dishevelled hair just made him more irresistible.

Leaning forward, she kissed him briefly on the cheek and quickly withdrew, too wary of betraying her longing for more. Old habits died hard, she thought, wishing she'd hugged Dante as she'd wanted.

'No!' Carlo crossly turned her head back. 'Like Paolo's mummy and daddy do!'

'Silly Mummy,' Dante murmured and kissed Miranda full on the lips.

She imagined that his mouth lingered a little on hers but then it was gone, leaving her feeling very shaky. She rose with a rustle of silk and hauled Carlo into her arms.

'I think,' she declared breathily, in case her son came up with any more intimate gestures that Paolo's parents might have indulged in, 'it's time for your bath and bedtime story.'

'No—!'

'Yes!' they chorused, and exchanged the conspiratorial smiles of parents the world over.

The instinctive communication between them made her feel good. It seemed that Dante's hostility had melted away after an afternoon and evening of sheer fun.

A child, she thought, can reach parts that nothing else can. And her hopes lifted several notches.

'I can get to the top of the stairs before you do,' announced Dante slyly.

'Can't!' yelled Carlo, and set off at a great pace, his face sweetly earnest in his determination, his little legs comically twinkling over the marble floor as they pretended to hurry after him.

It was as if a band of iron was squeezing her heart as she watched him and Dante together. The two males in her life. The two people she loved above everyone else. And she wanted their love more than anything else in the entire world.

She had to really work hard to overcome her reticence if she was to win Dante's heart. Biting her lip, she started up after them. So many obstacles, she thought soberly, lifting her skirts and taking two stairs at a time. A mountain to climb.

'I won! I won!'

Carlo's ecstatic face swam into her vision. A huge kiss was deposited clumsily on her knee and then a small, trusting hand slid into hers.

'You were very quick,' she praised, her voice shaky with the depths that her love could reach.

'Boats,' he declared simply, drawing her into the bathroom, where Dante, with his sleeves rolled up to the elbows, was checking the temperature of the water gushing from the tap.

'Yes, we'll get the boats in a minute,' she answered.

She knelt, like Dante, and made to help her son undress but was firmly pushed away.

'I do it. I do it!' he insisted.

I love you so much, she thought, watching in fond amusement as he struggled with his clothes. She glanced at Dante and her heart stopped for a moment. There was such adoration in his eyes for Carlo that it brought her near to tears.

Lightly she touched Dante's arm to show that she felt the same. When he looked at her it seemed that his eyes softened and warmed like dark, swirling chocolate. Her heart raced. He wanted to love her, she felt sure. Wanted to forget the past and, like her, he longed to be sure that these golden moments with Carlo would continue.

To encourage him she psyched herself up to slip her arm around his waist while she assessed the bath water with an expert eye.

'Deep enough, do you think?'

He kept staring at her. The way he had when they were lovers. Her brain seemed to be doing cartwheels.

'Deeper than you know,' he replied softly.

Her head continued to spin. Could he mean...?

'Up! Up!' demanded Carlo, pushing his wiry, naked body between them, and Dante let out a hiss of breath then lifted their son into the bath.

She wasn't sure what was happening to her—or to Dante. But she did know that Carlo was having fun and she and Dante were trying to get soap onto the wriggling child enthusiastically propelling his plastic boats around the choppy bath water.

There was a knock on the door and, just as she planted a

kiss on Carlo's merry mop of curls, Luca stepped into the bathroom.

'Excuse me,' he said politely. Then his eyes kindled at the sight of Carlo and Miranda, sinking each other's boats. He grinned. 'Er… The *contessa's* sister called to say that some of your clothes will be arriving by special messenger.'

'Oh, good. Thank you.' Miranda smiled at him as she dropped a protective towel over her crushed-silk skirt. She was delighted that Luca had unbent towards her a little. The power of a child to move men's hearts! she thought. 'Hey!' she protested, when Carlo took advantage of her inattention and craftily sat on her boat. 'You rascal!' she cried, pretending to be indignant and making her son collapse into a heap of giggles.

'I a rascal!' he declared in glee.

'And I adore you!'

Miranda kissed his neck enthusiastically and elicited squeals from Carlo with her fake nibbles of his shoulder.

''Dore me! 'Dore me!' Carlo cried.

Luca gave a polite little cough.

'Sorry!' Miranda flung him an apologetic grin. 'I just love bath time.'

'So do I, *Contessa*,' Luca said softly, his eyes warm as he watched Carlo.

'You have children?' she asked eagerly.

'Five. All boys.'

His pride was evident and she beamed to see it.

'All handsome, all a credit to their parents,' Dante provided.

Luca's smile stretched from ear to ear. 'Thank you, *Conte. Allora*, I had a further message from your sister, *Contessa*. She said that she would call you in a day or two to tell you of her purchases in Milan.'

Miranda raised her eyes to the ceiling. 'I hope the shops weren't cleaned out! Lizzie's never been given her head before.'

'She was very happy, *Contessa*,' Luca murmured tactfully.

'I'm sure she was! Well thank you for looking after her—'

'Yes, Luca,' interrupted Dante. 'We're grateful.' And to

Miranda's surprise, he continued after a slight hesitation, 'Like you, Lizzie lost her father when she was small, and her mother died when she was twelve. Miranda had her work cut out. But now we will all be Lizzie's parents, yes?'

The man's intelligent eyes were thoughtful as they rested on Miranda and she felt he understood what she had endured as the elder child.

'I understand,' he said gently, his face wreathed in smiles. 'Yes. We will watch over the young lady when she is here. Goodnight, *Conte, Contessa.*'

When Luca had slipped quietly away, Miranda put a hand on Dante's arm. 'That was nice of you. I hadn't realised you understood how tough it was for Lizzie.'

'And for you. I'm not blind, Miranda,' he answered, adding a little more warm water. He smiled at her. 'You'll have to live your childhood through Carlo, since you must have missed so much of your own.'

Their gazes locked and her pulses skittered about crazily. He swallowed, scooped up some suds and blew them at Carlo, then did the same to her. In the ensuing uproar her mind was in turmoil like her blood, which was pumping erratically around her taut body. And Dante's hands were shaking like hers.

'Like old times, isn't it?' she whispered unfairly.

'Uh.'

Frowning, he pushed back a lock of hair that had fallen onto his forehead, leaving it wet and frothy from the bubbles. In a tender, wifely gesture, Miranda reached up and flicked the froth away, her face close to his.

For a breathless moment she thought he might kiss her but then he sucked in a sharp rasp of air and busied himself with the soap and Carlo's grubby knees again.

To contain her urge to fling her arms around Dante and declare her love again, she picked up another bar of soap and attacked Carlo's neck and back. With every stroke she was chanting feverishly to herself,

'Dante loves me. He loves me not. Loves me, loves me not…'

''Ook, Mummy!'

'I'm looking, darling!' she whispered lovingly as Carlo intently soaped his father's arm.

Small, plump fingers then undid Dante's dress shirt. Miranda watched in silence, absorbing her son's touching concentration and Dante's laughing surrender to Carlo's solemn attentions.

'I'm very wet!' Dante protested to Carlo.

'I wet too!' he replied in glee.

'Well, I think it's time we both got dry again. I have a new story for you,' Dante said, hastily mopping up the water that had dripped to his navel.

Miranda tore her gaze away and lifted Carlo out, clean and sparkling. They both dried him, their eyes meeting over his sopping curls as he chattered happily.

On impulse, Miranda hugged her damp son's body to her, her eyes closing in silent thanks that she could see and touch and love him again. This was worth a million arguments, hours of cold hostility. Whatever Dante felt about her, whatever happened, she would withstand it because of these precious moments.

When she lifted her blurred eyes, blinking her spiky wet lashes, she met the full force of Dante's intense gaze. And she felt her limbs become watery.

Seeing her weakness, he gently turned Carlo around.

'I'll do your pyjamas for you,' he said softly, reaching for a pair decorated with trains.

Miranda watched as he slowly eased them on her son's little arms and legs, which were limp with fatigue now, the constant battering of chatter abruptly silenced.

'Up we go.'

Dante stood up and swung Carlo into his arms. Walking into his bedroom with Miranda following in a dream, he tenderly deposited their son in the great vastness of his bed and snuggled up beside him with a book.

'Mummy come too.'

Sleepily, Carlo lifted an arm and beckoned Miranda by repeatedly holding his palm flat and then curling his fingers up, a gesture that had always touched her heart.

This was what they had used to do, when Dante was home. 'A Carlo sandwich,' she recalled and Dante smiled. Obediently she scrambled up the other side of Carlo with a sensuous whisper of silk.

'Lovery Mummy,' Carlo murmured, stroking the material.

Lovely Mummy! It was wonderful to hear those words again. She kissed her son's soft cheek, awash with love, and he burrowed contentedly between them. She lay there while Dante read the story and Carlo stopped fidgeting and grew steadily limper.

The bed had a lingering fragrance. She inhaled it and the essence of Dante's male body permeated every part of her being. His arm, slung protectively around Carlo, was touching her. Wanting to maintain that contact, she leaned into it, her cheek sliding against his skin.

Her hand curved around Carlo's head in a tender caress. She could feel elation rising inside her and risked a glance up at Dante as he read the story. After a moment he met her gaze and faltered, his voice tailing away into a throaty whisper.

'We would be fools,' she whispered softly, seeing that Carlo was asleep, 'to throw all of this away by sticking to a cold-blooded business arrangement.'

He put down the book and in silence he studied Carlo's small face. Miranda held her breath, knowing he was considering her suggestion. For them both, this child of theirs was so important that they would do anything to make him happy.

Carlo. Adoringly she gazed at him. Twin black fringes lay heavily on the sweet, olive-skinned face. The cupid's bow mouth was no longer laughing but soft and crumpled in sleep. The energetic bomb of a body had become floppy and heavy. Her heart filled with love.

Slowly Dante eased away and stood up. Without looking at her he said quietly,

'Time to talk.'

Nerves jangling, she nodded and slid from the bed, following Dante to the door. Then a few feet along the landing he turned, muttering, 'Baby monitor…' and as she sidestepped out of the way, so did he. They collided. The rest was a blur.

But she found herself somehow in his arms and his mouth was hard on hers, driving hard as if violent passions were being released.

Fire roared through her body as if she'd been ignited. Everything would be all right! she thought exultantly as his hands pulled her hard to him, echoing her desperate need to feel every inch of him, to be so close that not a hair's breadth lay between them.

'Miranda, Miranda!' he breathed into her eager mouth.

She felt she was soaring to the sky. Her hands locked around his beautiful head and she could feel the clean silk of his hair and smell his familiar smell of subtle vanilla and man.

Her straps were being eased down. His mouth wandered hotly over her naked shoulders, skimming over her skin in tense, passionate kisses. She felt delicate fingers slipping into her lacy bra, his lips exploring the deep V of her cleavage.

She let out a gasp and then a little whimper of pleasure when he lightly touched a straining nipple. Forcing his head up, she kissed him deeply, luxuriating in his expert touch, the fierce stabs of desire, and the hard promise of his body.

At some time she must have torn open his shirt because her hands could now move unhindered over his muscular chest, every inch of which had become familiar to her. And her fingers lingered over his heavily beating heart because it was a miraculous confirmation that he, too, must be experiencing a wild and unstoppable arousal.

Her conscious mind no longer operated. It was as if she was intoxicated by the drug of love. He could make her forget everything when he made love to her. She had no will of her own, only a pagan drive to become part of him.

Fiercely demanding, she pushed him against the wall and

pressed herself harder against the contours of his body, moving in the sinuous way that always made him lose control.

Almost immediately he bucked and groaned, lifting her skirts and curving his hands beneath her taut buttocks to lift her up.

Wantonly she tucked her naked legs around his waist and pulled off her top. As she did so, Dante buried his mouth in her breasts, his fingers busy with the fastening of her bra.

She took his face between her hands and kissed him with slow and tender passion, shuddering when the lace barrier had been removed and they were skin to skin.

Her senses were filled with him, her heart hammering loudly in her ears.

'I love you! I love you!' she breathed.

And then he froze. Jerked back, a stunned expression on his face.

She shouldn't have said that! She'd scared him away! Wide-eyed, she stared at him as he slowly lowered her to the ground, his eyes black and fathomless.

Her skirts fell back into place with a sensual whisper but it was lost on Dante. He was going to reject her and call her a sex-crazed harlot, she thought hysterically. And felt a feral wail of misery and frustration rise up within her.

CHAPTER NINE

'DANTE! Dante!'

She blinked. Someone was calling from downstairs.

'It's Guido!' Dante grated, looking angry.

Though whether he was annoyed with himself for succumbing to her, or with Guido for choosing that moment to arrive, she didn't know.

'What…?' She swallowed, to lubricate her throat, and then frantically snatched up her bra. 'What's he doing here?'

Hastily dealing with the buttons of his shirt, he shot her an unreadable look.

'I expect he's brought your things from England. You'd better tidy yourself up,' he rasped, smoothing down his ruffled hair and avoiding eye contact. He pushed open a door, to reveal a bedroom. 'It would look odd if you didn't come down to thank him.'

Biting her lip, she scooped up her top and pulled it on, following him into the bedroom as he checked his appearance in the dressing-table mirror. His eyes were black and liquid, his lips parted to allow his shortened breath to escape.

'Dante?' she said uncertainly.

'Please,' he muttered, closing his eyes. 'I have to come back to earth.'

Miranda felt a sudden stab of elation. Maybe, she thought with rising hope, he had pulled away from her because he'd heard his brother calling—and not for any other reason.

'We are married,' she pointed out.

Still avoiding her eyes, he said softly, 'Yes. But we have a guest.'

'You look terribly flushed,' she observed in amusement.

'We've been playing with Carlo. That would flush anyone!'

With a shaky grin he swept past her. 'Come down as quickly as you can.'

'Hmm. You'll need to wipe the lipstick from your neck first,' she murmured.

He whirled, frowning at the mirror, as Guido's voice echoed through the hall.

'Damn!' Dante muttered. 'I didn't notice—!'

'Come here.'

Miranda drew a small handkerchief from her pocket. He hesitated, then strode over to her. Reaching up on tiptoe, she gently rubbed at the offending mark. Then kissed him on the mouth.

He groaned and his lips softened beneath hers. 'I've got to go!' he whispered. Then called, 'Guido! I'm coming!' and hurried from the room.

Light-hearted, humming a little tune, Miranda ran into her quarters as if treading on air. She refreshed her lipstick and brushed her hair and smiled at her reflection, thinking how different she looked with her eyes sparkling and her skin glowing from a new, inner radiance.

Still humming under her breath, she flew down the stairs and headed for the sound of voices.

'Guido!' she cried, managing to smile at Dante's much-loved younger brother.

Curly-haired, shorter than Dante and stockier, he came towards her, his arms open wide in greeting.

'Miranda! You look sensational!' he purred.

And something odd happened. She looked into his eyes and felt a spurt of fear travel right through her. It took all her will-power not to take a step back.

'Thank you!' she said breathily and found herself wrapped in Guido's bear hug. Panic screamed through her. She began to breathe harshly as he kissed her enthusiastically on her hot cheeks, his body too intimate with hers. 'Hey! Put me down!' she cried, choking back the nausea and pretending to be amused. But his mocking eyes told her that he knew she wasn't comfortable. 'What will my husband say?'

'I'm family!' Guido protested, but he did let her go.

Miranda had to get away before she was sick right there. 'Was that Carlo?' she fudged, her head on one side as though she'd heard a cry. 'I'd better go up. Shan't be long.'

In her bathroom, after a rather undignified scuttle up the stairs on incredibly shaky legs, she cooled her face with cold water and stood with her eyes shut, mastering her nausea.

What an odd reaction! She'd never felt like this before! She'd eaten nothing strange to make her sick...

She froze. Her eyes snapped open in shock. No. She couldn't be! Not...*pregnant?* Would that explain the odd feelings?

Her period was overdue. And she had always been regular. But there had only been that one occasion—at least a month ago—when she and Dante had made love, she calculated. He had been away so much. It seemed unlikely that she'd become pregnant then, but it was possible, of course. It only took the once.

Pale and dizzy, she clutched at the basin, not sure whether to be delighted or horrified. The last thing she wanted was for Dante to come back to her just because she was carrying his child. She needed him to choose *her*, not because she was producing another addition to the Severini dynasty—the heir and a spare.

Her hand strayed to her flat, hard stomach and she found herself smiling blissfully to think that Dante's child might be already growing inside her. It would be lovely, she thought dreamily. And prayed that she *was* pregnant. However, if she was, then she would keep it a secret until she knew for sure that Dante really cared for her.

But where, she wondered, could she go to get a pregnancy test, without half of Italy knowing? She giggled, excited and happy again.

High on adrenaline and glowing with delight, she descended the stairs and drifted into the salon. The two men stopped talking as if they'd been discussing her but their admiring expressions told her that she looked strikingly different from a few moments ago.

Yet it only took a leer from Guido to throw her off balance and unnerve her again. He seemed to be getting under her skin though she didn't know why.

Deliberately she chose to sit as far away from him as possible, settling herself on a Renaissance chaise longue beneath a wall displaying portraits of medieval Severini cardinals.

Dante brought her a drink. 'You look wonderful,' he murmured.

Her starry eyes flicked up to his and she couldn't stop the radiant smile from lighting up her whole face.

'Thank you,' she whispered back.

Then, as he gazed into her eyes, a slight frown formed, drawing his black brows together as if he was puzzled. Could he tell? she wondered, absently taking a gulp of the champagne. And then she wished she hadn't in case she really was pregnant. She put the glass down on the gilt table and concentrated on appearing normal.

'What bright eyes you have!' Guido drawled. 'You look like an advert for eye drops. Or something.'

Eye drops? She blinked. And understood the cause of Dante's frown. 'I am happy,' she said calmly. 'I don't need artificial substances.'

'I should hope not!' Guido declared in rather overdone horror. 'I've been to too many parties where people disappeared into bathrooms for a snort of cocaine and came back with suspiciously bright eyes.'

'Miranda wouldn't dream of using drugs here.' Dante spoke with firmness and she smiled at him gratefully.

'No. I wouldn't,' she said softly. 'It would destroy our relationship and that's too precious to risk.'

Dante visibly relaxed and she realised how tense he'd been. It worried her that Guido was sowing seeds of doubt in Dante's mind. And she couldn't fathom why.

'Guido has brought some of your possessions from England,' Dante said, adroitly changing the subject.

'I gather you were the special messenger, Guido. Thank you,' she managed to say to him. 'I appreciate your efforts.'

'No problem,' he said airily. 'I had some help from Lizzie. Some pad, eh?'

He leaned back in his deep armchair. His narrowed eyes scanned the richly decorated room, the carved ceiling, marble fireplace and elegant furniture with greedy approval.

'You know Lizzie?' she said, surprised.

Guido grinned rather nastily and gave a suggestive little chuckle that made her flinch and shrink into the depths of the upholstery.

'As well as I know you,' he said with a smirk.

Not well, then, she thought with relief. Although Dante doted on his brother, she'd never quite taken to him. There was something sly and self-seeking about the guy. The last thing she wanted was for the impressionable Lizzie to get involved with him.

She looked at his stubby hands and inexplicably found herself shuddering. The pleasure of her possible pregnancy had been completely overshadowed by her irrational dislike of Guido.

'I asked Lizzie to sort out a few must-have items for you,' Dante explained to her, 'and to contact Guido so that he could bring them over. The rest will come overland. I hope that's all right?'

'Yes. Fine,' she said brightly. And forced herself to address Guido. 'How long will you be staying?'

Lazily the dark eyes lingered on her with such boldness that it felt as if he were ripping off her clothes. Stupid, she told herself. He was young, good-looking and virile, and probably gave all women the glad eye.

'A few days or so,' Guido drawled, his lips wet and seemingly bloody from the red wine he was drinking. 'If that's acceptable.'

'Of course.'

She tried to sound enthusiastic for Dante's sake but her

instincts were to recoil from him as if he were a venomous snake.

Maybe she had become super-sensitive—a downside of pregnancy, perhaps? Guido hadn't affected her like this in all the time she'd known him at the London office. She knew his reputation with women from office gossip and that he had a rather cavalier attitude of 'love 'em and leave 'em'. Although she'd never liked him, these feelings of extreme revulsion were entirely new.

'The weather's vile in England,' he confided. 'I look forward to swimming and sunbathing by the pool with you both.'

The thought of exposing her body to Guido's lecherous stare almost made her throw up. Hastily she took a sip of her drink and put it down again guiltily as Dante threw his brother an indulgent look.

'We'll catch up on business, Guido, then we can all have a lazy day chilling out.' He turned to Miranda. 'You haven't christened that new bikini yet, have you?'

Vowing to plead a headache—or at least to wear the boring one-piece—she stretched her lips in the shape of a smile.

'That's for your eyes only,' she said shakily.

Guido's eyebrow shot up. 'Sounds interesting! Bit revealing, is it?'

She gagged and covered that up with a series of coughs while Dante playfully punched his brother's shoulder.

They began to discuss their plans for the next day. Either it was her imagination, or Guido was watching her like a hawk. She shivered as his gaze wandered to her cleavage and it seemed that something vile was crawling over her skin. She couldn't stand any more of this.

'Look,' she said, standing up suddenly and prompting the men to leap from their seats again. 'I hope you don't think this is rude, and I know you've only just arrived, Guido, but I'm very tired. I think I'll go to bed or I won't be able to cope with Carlo in the morning.' She flashed a smile at both of them, though only with Dante did her eyes warm as well. 'Goodnight, darling.'

Deliberately she walked over, put her arms around Dante's neck and kissed him tenderly on the mouth. His arms closed around her, his mouth hardened its pressure for a brief moment as if he wanted to deepen the kiss and then he released her.

'Goodnight, Miranda,' he said softly.

She smiled. Inviting him with her eyes. 'Don't stay up late,' she whispered, her hand lingering on his chest.

'No,' he promised. 'I won't.'

She sensed that Guido was tense and disapproving and forced herself to walk quickly past him in case he expected a goodnight kiss too.

''Night,' she said to him with a casual wave, and headed a little unsteadily for the door.

'I'll just nip out and tell you what I've brought, in case you want some of it upstairs now,' Guido said, shooting after her.

Her stomach somersaulted and she hurried into the hall.

'Don't bother. I can manage with what I have,' she said sharply.

But he was right behind her and she had to increase her pace even more to avoid his cloying aftershave and the little prickles of fear that attacked her whenever he was close. She was part way up the stairs when he spoke, calling up from the hallway.

'Dante tells me,' he murmured, 'that you and he have patched up your differences. Does that mean he's forgiven you for being unfaithful?'

'I wasn't unfaithful!' she cried indignantly. 'I told you that,' she reminded him, 'when you came around to see me after he disappeared and I rang your office to see if he was there—'

'Well,' Guido said with a shrug, 'you have to admit that even by your version of events, it looks bad. I think he's a saint to put family honour second and I told him so, just now.'

Annoyed, she turned around to face him, crushing her panic with an effort.

'We're sorting our own lives out, Guido,' she said coldly, afraid that his interference might ruin everything. 'I think you can leave it to us to work out a solution.'

Guido looked her up and down in a rather insulting way and she couldn't prevent herself from shuddering.

'I can see why he wants to forgive, even if he can't ever forget. He'd be a fool not to want you back in his bed. That body of yours would tempt a monk. Though I imagine he'll loathe himself for giving in to his urges. Dante's got high morals.' He heaved a melodramatic sigh. 'I don't suppose he'll ever be able to put your infidelity out of his mind. Every time he makes love to you, he'll be wondering about your lover and how his performance matches up—'

'I think you've said enough!' she whispered, white with anger.

'I am concerned for my brother's welfare.' He paused. Then asked, 'Are you one hundred per cent sure there was no man with you that night?'

She stared, unable to answer. She had a flashback of hot breath on her face, those rough hands...

Miranda's eyes grew huge with horror. No. She wasn't sure. A shudder went through her at his look of triumph.

'There you are!' he murmured. 'And one other thing worries me.' He looked up at her slyly. 'Are you hoping to milk him for all he's worth?'

She gasped. 'How dare you?' she whispered, hoarse with fury.

Guido shrugged. 'I can't see any other reason for you to hang around. No normal woman would be able to stand being touched by a man who doesn't give a damn about her.'

'I only have your word for that,' she said thickly.

'On the contrary. You have his.'

Guido came closer, holding her captive with his intense gaze. Frozen to the spot on the stairs, she knew he was going to tell her something she didn't want to hear but she felt compelled to listen, to know the whole truth.

'Why do you say that, Guido?' she croaked.

'He's just told me. He was laughing, saying that now he had the inheritance, the title and his son. And the services of a sexy woman whenever he chose to snap his fingers.'

'I—I don't believe you!' she rasped, wishing she could sound more convinced.

'I'm the only one who tells you the truth,' Guido assured her. 'You knew nothing of our uncle's will or its conditions until I explained them. Dante kept that a secret from you. I am the only person you can trust to tell it how it is. Remember that, Miranda, when—'

'Do you need a hand to carry any luggage up?' Dante called and soon appeared in the doorway of the salon.

'I don't want *anything* that's down there in the hall,' she said, making a point of including Guido in the sweep of her gaze. Her head reeled. She didn't know what to believe now.

'I think I'll come up, anyway.' Dante came forward and slapped his brother on the back. 'Your room's second on the left. See you in the morning for that chat about business. Help yourself to whatever you want.'

Guido's eyes gleamed and rested briefly on Miranda. 'Generous of you,' he said with a low laugh. 'Thanks for the offer. I will do just that.'

And she felt her spine ice over. The brothers hugged and said their goodnights. Sick to the stomach and unreasonably scared, she turned and began to make her way slowly up the stairs.

Guido was up to something. He had taken against her, though she couldn't understand why.

And yet she couldn't confide her feelings to Dante. He had always been protective of his younger brother. Perhaps she should learn a little more about Guido, discover what made him tick.

Dante bounded up to her side and his arm drew her close. Gratefully she looked up, shaken by the tenderness of his expression.

'You look pale,' he murmured. And raised an enquiring eyebrow. 'Are you really tired?'

Her eyes kindled with hope. He wanted to make love to her. But he would, wouldn't he? A man steeped in sensuality, who needed sex...

'No!' she admitted. 'I just didn't want to spend the whole night chatting with Guido.'

'You'd rather sleep?' he teased, his voice low and seductive.

How could she resist him? And yet she must, while her doubts about Dante were so strong. She had to find out if Guido was lying when he claimed his brother merely wanted a sex toy to play with.

'I was thinking of something more important,' she began croakily.

'Me too. I thought…we could play games.' His hand slipped to her buttocks so that she could feel the sway of her own hips.

'Like?' she queried helplessly, suddenly husky.

'Hide and seek. Kiss chase,' he murmured. 'Hunt the—'

'Dante!' she cried in mock reproof.

He chuckled and his lips sought her neck. He pushed open the double doors to his suite and spun her around, leaning against the door jamb and kissing her more thoroughly. But still she wanted to be sure that this wasn't just sex. It had to be more.

'We were going to talk,' she reminded him breathlessly, pushing back a little.

'Later. I want you.'

Joy filled her heart. His head dipped but she ducked beneath his arms, emerging flushed and trembling a foot or so away, in his sitting room.

'*Please!*'

He took one look at her set face and quietly closed the doors behind them. 'What is it?' he asked warily.

She had to be direct. To eradicate all doubts. So before she had cold feet, she hurled a blunt question,

'Why do you want me?'

He raised an eyebrow. 'Isn't that obvious?'

'Sex. Any other reason?' she asked shakily.

He sighed. 'Several.'

'You said I was soiled goods. That—'

His mouth twisted. 'Miranda,' he said throatily. 'Come and sit down.'

Taking her arm, he led her to a sofa. Sitting beside her, he turned her stubborn, unhappy face to his, kissed her gently on the lips and then held both her hands in his firm grip.

'I distinctly remember you saying that our marriage had been based on sex, not love—' she persisted miserably.

'Well, yes,' he said, plummeting her spirits to the very depths. 'I was referring to you. I thought at that time that you'd married me for my money. I feel sure now that isn't true. I believe you did love me.'

Her solemn eyes were fixed on his and she tried to grasp the implications of what he was saying.

'So…you didn't mean that *you'd* had sex without love?' she croaked.

'No, never,' he muttered. 'It would have been easier for me if that had been true.'

A radiant smile broke out over her face. He had loved her in those early days and Guido had been mistaken—or he had lied. Now, why would he do that? And her brother-in-law had suggested that Dante was still using her.

'I—I had the impression you'd been discussing me with Guido when I came in,' she said nervously.

'I was,' Dante admitted. 'He asked me if I was happy and I told him that I had everything I wanted—'

'The inheritance? Carlo? A sexy woman at your beck and call to warm your bed?' she flung in distress.

Dante looked shocked. 'I would never describe you like that to anyone, even my brother!' he declared. 'Is that how you see it, Miranda?'

'I don't know what to think!' she cried passionately. 'You keep giving off different signals and it's driving me mad! How do I know where I stand? Tell me honestly. How do you feel about me right at this minute?'

'As confused as you are,' he growled. 'Miranda… You evoke such emotions in me! Such a conflict of feelings… When I thought up this proposition—that we should live together for Carlo's sake—I believed I despised and hated you so much that a business arrangement wouldn't be a problem. But I've discovered that you care about Carlo very much. That means everything to me. It has changed the way I think of you.'

He lowered his gaze, watching his thumbs stroking the backs of her hands as if mesmerised by the action. But when he lifted his eyes again, she saw that they were bright and intense.

Little shivers were running up and down her spine. It still wasn't enough, she thought. And, throwing caution to the wind, she asked breathlessly,

'*How* do you think of me now?'

He pushed a hand through his hair. 'Torn,' he said. 'You see, I've never been able to reconcile what I knew of you with the evidence that was presented to me—'

'Whoever poisoned your mind was mistaken!' she flared. 'Something strange happened that night you found me—'

'Don't, Miranda!' he said fiercely. 'I don't want to think of that time. It was the worst night of my life.'

'And mine!' she whispered, her eyes huge with the horror of it.

'We have to put it behind us.' His voice grated. She realised how hard this was for him. He couldn't forget what he'd seen. 'This is now. We must try to forget the past—'

'*Can* you forget it?'

He struggled with his conscience. 'No,' he growled finally. And, seeing her flinch, he added, 'It keeps coming back to haunt me—as it does you. It's hard to erase such a traumatic moment from one's mind.'

'I know!' she muttered fervently.

'We'll get through it. Together,' he said quietly and her eyes flicked up to his in hope. 'I have to tell you, Miranda,' he said hotly. 'I've been in torment ever since you arrived. Try as I might, I can't stop thinking of you. Can't keep away from you. I want to touch you every time I see you. To kiss your beautiful mouth. Like that... And again...and again... I can't stay detached. I want you.' His mouth drifted over hers again. 'I want to be with you. For us to live as man and wife.'

'Because you want me in your bed?' she asked soberly, her heart thudding hard.

'Yes!' he hissed. 'And…'

She held her breath. Waited for an age. Then had to prompt. 'And?' she asked, hoping, hoping…

'And because I want *you*,' he said huskily.

She looked at him for a moment. This wasn't the time for self-delusion.

'Do you mean "want" as in "love"?'

Again she waited. He seemed to be making up his mind. She panicked. Surely he knew whether he loved her or not? The hesitation was too protracted. She'd rather the truth—

'Fool that I am. I've hated you for this. For making me your prisoner. But the answer is yes,' he muttered, and pulled her to him.

They both went a little crazy. By the time they hurried out of the sitting room and passed through Dante's bedroom where Carlo slept, many of their clothes had been scattered in a trail around the sitting room's carpet.

And once they reached her suite, they hungrily stripped one another, not even waiting before they reached her bedroom but sinking to the thick carpet in a tangle of arms and legs as if they had been starved of love and sex for years.

She couldn't get enough of him. Couldn't get close enough, her body arching and straining in an effort to melt into his, the force of her desperate passion driving her to demand to be kissed and touched here, and here, and there…

And he obliged, his ardour matching hers, his hunger as great. She was being devoured, her body sliding slickly against his, her skin tingling from his sensational caresses, her mouth ever ready to taste and bite and lick and savour the essence of the man she loved with every beat of her pounding heart.

'*Now!*' she groaned, when he tormented her with his gentle fingers, even though she had long ago liquefied for him.

His tongue explored. She sobbed with need. Grabbed his hair and made him move up her body. He took one look at her impassioned face and groaned.

Then her eyes closed because she felt the silken heat of him as he entered her and she held him to her, hardly believing that they were together again. Her heart soared and she began to float as she always did, whimpering a little, moving voluptuously beneath his body as he began to drive rhythmically inside her and the sweet pleasure filled every cell with pulsing energy.

He whispered brokenly to her, Italian words she didn't know but which sounded tender and loving, and she spoke to him, crying out her love, her adoration, his beloved name.

The climb to orgasm was fiercer and deeper than anything she had ever known. For seemingly hours she clung to its peaks, her body responding feverishly to Dante's erotic attentions. He held her there, coaxing and murmuring, his voice and body filling her entire mind with profound pleasure.

'Look at me!' he rasped. '*Me!* Say my name!'

Her drowsy, drugged eyes flickered open a little.

'Dante!' she whispered and he groaned.

She watched with love and rivers of sweet pain as he gazed down at her and climaxed, only closing his own eyes in ecstasy at the last moment. Shaken by the intensity of their lovemaking, they slowly came back to sanity. And, tucked close together, they lay in contented peace.

This was true happiness, she thought dreamily. She, Dante, Carlo, their new baby, living together, loving and laughing, the years passing by in a daze of delight.

Having once lost them both, she wasn't going to lose them again. She and Dante would grow old, watching Carlo and, she thought with a blissful smile, this child, other children, ride their first bike, go to their first dance, shine at school, university, marry, have children of their own...

Nothing, she vowed fiercely, nothing would take that future from her. It was everything she had always wanted. To experience the deepest, most profound love. And a family of her own to love her too. Heaven. Sheer heaven.

Sometime in the early hours the spasms of a panic attack woke her, and she came spiralling out of her nightmare in a desperate attempt to escape it, jerking awake with a shuddering start.

Knowing that Dante was fast asleep, she clenched her teeth and fought the nausea and terror of her dream, so horribly fresh in her mind.

The stinking breath. The bruising fingers biting into her arms, the strong thighs—Oh, God! she thought, her eyes wide with disgust at the realisation—those hard male thighs were naked, the dark hairs abrading her delicate skin!

In the darkness she felt her muscles knot with panic as the memory was replayed in her brain and *everything*, everything came flooding back with unwelcome clarity. This time she could actually see the face that loomed towards her for a travesty of a kiss while she lay there, dumbly waiting for it.

It was a face she recognised. Her breath caught in her throat. Lungs ceased to work. Body became paralysed with horror.

It was Guido!

Guido's eyes. His triumphant mouth. He was laughing as she lay there inert, unable, it seemed, to stop him. She recalled that at that moment a glass had clinked. His impatient hand had pushed it away and she remembered turning her head very very slowly and seeing two glasses and the bottle of champagne. And then she'd blacked out.

Appalled, she let out short, desperate shots of air from her bursting lungs. Had she been drunk? High on cocaine? Was that why she'd been so passive and accepting?

And…what had happened next? She searched her memory. Nothing further came. Only horrible suspicions.

'Oh, dear heaven!' she whispered. 'Please, no!'

She couldn't have let him… Wouldn't have. Not in a million years. And yet… The evidence was there. Stark and frightening, damning her horribly.

Of course that was why Guido had behaved so oddly. Why she'd reacted to him with such instinctive loathing. He'd known what had happened and he had wanted to prevent Dante from associating with her...

'Darling?'

'*Ohh!*' She jumped like a scalded cat.

Found herself in Dante's arms, his voice murmuring in lyrical Italian. 'Had that nightmare again?' he asked gruffly.

All she could do was nod, without speaking. She didn't deserve his sympathy. Maybe she wasn't worthy of him. Maybe she had betrayed him. There had been no rape. But perhaps she had, in her fuddled haze, allowed Guido to—to...

Despairing, she broke down and wept. Dante held her, stroking her hair, telling her it would be all right, he was there now. Which made it worse. Sickness surged up from her stomach and she wrenched herself free, stumbling blindly to the bathroom, where she retched till she collapsed on the floor in a trembling heap.

Her face was being wiped. Blankets wrapped around her. She was being held securely again.

Oh, how painful that was! She had won an admission from Dante that he couldn't live without her. But she had no right to stay with him. She had let his brother paw her, and probably worse. She closed her eyes, remembering what Guido had said. That he knew Lizzie as well as he knew *her*.

Oh, Lizzie! she thought in horror. Her sister had to be told. Warned...

'Come on. Back to bed.' Dante lifted her up in his arms and she was too weak to object. 'You'll see a doctor in the morning,' he declared, his fingers gently smoothing the furrow between her brows.

'Yes,' she whispered. A doctor... She stiffened the length of her body.

'What is it?' Dante asked her anxiously. 'Another part of the nightmare come back?' Somehow in the depths of her shock she managed to nod. 'You're safe with me. I'll look after you,' he murmured, kissing her forehead.

But she was far from safe and there was no way he'd look after her if he knew the truth.

Because if she was pregnant, then she could be carrying Guido's child.

CHAPTER TEN

To HER relief, they were up before Guido, who had left a terrible mess in the salon for the maid to clear up. Two bottles of champagne had rolled onto the floor, a glass had been smashed and there was evidence of carelessly eaten food on the cushions and on the rich brocade of a chair. Plus heel marks where he'd rested dirty shoes on a sofa.

The offending shoes lay carelessly discarded on the Aubusson rug, together with a pair of socks which had been hastily pulled off.

Miranda, pale and drawn after a virtually sleepless night, said nothing to Dante about this. Her stomach turned at the thought of clearing up his mess, so she sought out the maid in the servants' quarters and made her regret understood, before joining Dante and Carlo for breakfast.

'You don't look too good, darling,' he said, hurrying over to her in concern.

'Headache,' she muttered sickly.

'I'll see to Carlo.' He ushered her into a chair and fussed over her until she was settled. 'Have some *tisane*.' He poured some camomile tea for her and pushed the fruit in her direction. 'Eat something, *mia cara*,' he instructed.

She nibbled a strawberry and then another. Watching the two of them with tightly concealed misery, she tried to imagine life without them. But the prospect was so bleak, so appalling, that she shied away from it.

A short time ago everything had seemed rosy. Now she was in despair again.

She didn't want to lose Carlo, or Dante. Her child needed her. If she did the honourable thing and left now, then Carlo would suffer. She thought of the happiness she'd felt just be-

133

fore she'd fallen asleep and tasted bitter gall in her throat as
her dreams for the future crumbled to dust.

Her hands clenched into tight fists beneath the damask cloth.
Some day soon she would have to tell Dante what had happened that night. She would have to throw herself on his
mercy.

But would he believe her when she revealed the identity of
the man who'd got her drunk and incapable? She chewed the
corner of her lip, unsure whether to name Guido or not. Dante
adored his brother. She'd be destroying that love.

'You'll get permanent wrinkles if you keep frowning like
that,' Dante said gently, his hand closing over hers.

She looked down at it and the tears filled her eyes.
Doggedly forcing them back, she managed a pathetic little
smile.

'You wouldn't be attracted to me then,' she muttered, trying
to joke.

His grip tightened. He lifted her hand, turned it over and
kissed her fingers. 'My passion is for *you*, the person you are.'
He grinned. 'It's a bonus that you're beautiful, but I'll still
want you, wrinkles or not.'

How ironic. Now she was certain of his commitment to her,
now that he was actually declaring it, she was poised to have
it slip through her fingers.

Maybe she wasn't pregnant at all, she mused. It was very
early yet. She'd say nothing until she'd had the chance to do
a test—and that meant perhaps a trip to Como town, where
there was no chance of anyone knowing who she was.

But if she *was* pregnant... She trembled, torn between the
joy of carrying a baby that might be Dante's, and the misery
of mothering Guido's child, which would be born from her
stupidity and Guido's lust. How would she ever *know*?

She shuddered. With the prospect of losing what she had
so recently and joyously gained, she did the only thing possible. She grimly retreated back into the hard shell which had
protected her so well in the past.

'I'll pop up and do my teeth,' she said coolly, withdrawing her hand. 'Meet you and Carlo in the hall.'

'No problem,' he said happily, unaware of the turmoil in her tormented heart. 'I'll take him to nursery if you're not up to it.'

She didn't want to miss a moment with her child. 'No. I want to come. The fresh air will probably help.'

In the doorway an unstoppable force made her turn around. He was laughing with Carlo, laughing the way someone did when life was perfect and there were no worries on the horizon.

If only he knew! Feeling as though she carried enough burdens for the two of them, she slowly trudged to her room, sealing her heart as she went, shutting all access to her emotions.

It all depended on the pregnancy test. If it was negative then she'd tell Dante what had happened and they'd revert to their original plan: the business arrangement. It was the best she could expect.

If it was positive... She let out a sob. It would crucify her to keep silent, to let Dante assume he was the father of her child and to shower it with love, when it might be Guido's baby instead. So she would have to tell him of her doubts. She shuddered, envisaging his fury.

Would he then force her to leave? The pain sliced at her like sword thrusts and it was all she could do not to cry out loud. She was a survivor, she told herself. She would come out of this. One step at a time. She *must* get that test done— if it wasn't too early to tell, yet.

Her stomach rolled with fear but she doggedly concentrated on concealing her turbulent feelings. And for Carlo's sake, she shaped a bright smile on her face and went downstairs again.

It was a cloudy day and the lake had a heavy, metallic sheen. All the time she chatted with Dante and Carlo, she felt the sky pressing down on her and the weight of guilt crushing her spirits.

But she was used to hiding her state of mind and Dante

seemed so happy and carefree that he didn't notice anything. He kept mentioning Guido and telling Carlo that they'd all be doing various activities together, and her guts shrivelled at the thought. Guido wasn't the kind of person she wanted around Carlo. Her son wasn't going to be influenced by such a man!

'See you later, darling,' she said softly, near to tears as she hugged her little boy.

'*Certo!*' he replied, and they all laughed.

'Guido and I will give you Italian lessons to keep up with Carlo,' Dante said with a chuckle, waving goodbye to Carlo.

'No. Just you, please,' she said quickly, and Dante grinned, hugging her close.

'We'll start with parts of the body,' he murmured, as they strolled hand in hand down the street.

'Dante! You'll behave and teach me practical things.'

'That's what I was intending!' he murmured.

She loved him. Oh, she loved him so much... 'Look at the view,' she said, giving a reason for stopping. Her heart was pounding so hard she had no breath to walk.

'Wonderful.' But he was looking at her.

'The mountains, Dante!' she reproved, agony tearing into her stomach.

Why did he have to be so attentive and lovable right now? He was making it harder for her.

His arm came around her shoulders. From their vantage position at the top of the steep cobbled steps, they could see the jagged mountain peaks shrouded in veils of cloud. Below, a water skier was creating curls of white in the silver lake.

'Guido,' he identified, surprising her.

She watched the small, distant figure executing some stylish turns. 'He's very good,' she managed to say. This was her chance. She might learn a little about Dante's brother—something to explain why he was hell-bent on hurting her. 'Tell me about him,' she encouraged, though the words stuck in her throat.

Dante looked pleased. 'It's good to see him enjoying himself, poor devil,' he said sympathetically. 'He had a hard time as a child.'

Miranda shot him a quick glance. 'Oh? Why?'

He wrinkled his nose. 'Favouritism, I'm afraid. Both Mama and Papa favoured me. So did my uncle. It must have been crushing for him. I was the elder brother, with all the advantages. You know,' he said, waving his hands expansively, 'first bike, first to be allowed a glass of wine, to stay out late.'

'Perhaps,' she said quietly, 'you were favoured because you were more lovable.'

'No!' Dante looked aghast at the idea. 'Because I was the heir. The firstborn. That made me special in my parents' eyes. I shared my things with Guido but it wasn't the same as being given preference.'

They walked on. Her mind churned with ideas. 'He must have been jealous of you,' she said slowly. And yes, she'd noticed envy in Guido's eyes when he'd realised what Dante had inherited.

'Well, he wouldn't be human if he wasn't!' Dante laughed.

'Did he have many friends?' she asked, remembering how Guido had annoyed her colleagues by muscling in on their leisure activities.

'Not many,' Dante admitted. 'Being older and stronger, I was always having to protect him from being bullied. Other kids kept picking fights with him.'

'For no reason at all?' she said drily, knowing perfectly well why Guido had been roughed up. He was a nasty piece of work.

'They claimed he'd thumped them first or he'd stolen things from them.' Dante's face darkened. 'But Guido said they were lying. Naturally I believed him. I knew he'd never risk the family name by stealing.'

She wavered between telling him some time in the near future that his brother was a liar and had betrayed him, or remaining silent forever.

'You love him very much.'

'Yes,' he said gently. 'I do. I feel protective. I've had all the advantages in life. At school I had more success—and at university. My uncle was childless. He became a surrogate father when my own father died but he never had much time for my brother. Guido has suffered because of me—especially,' he said with a rueful smile, 'where women are concerned.'

Miranda felt muscles in her body twist into knots. This was the key to Guido's behaviour, she felt sure.

'What…do you mean?' she asked, her throat constricting.

'I was never short of dates,' he explained a little awkwardly. 'I realised then that it was because I was a "catch". A man with a glittering future. That,' he said frankly, 'is why I didn't tell you about my expectations. I wanted you to love me for myself.'

'I did. I do,' she said quietly.

He squeezed her hand. 'And I count myself fortunate because of that. Poor Guido. Being the younger brother without any particular prospects, he seemed to find it harder to make any kind of lasting relationship.'

'I see.'

It didn't surprise her. She didn't imagine that Guido would treat women well. Shortly after she'd started work at Severini's she'd walked into the ladies' cloakroom at the office and had overheard one of the typists complaining about Guido's roughness. She'd been showing her bruises to two other typists when they realised Miranda was there. Since she was Dante's secretary and might tell tales, they'd clammed up, but she'd been troubled.

And yet she'd said nothing, deciding that the typist should be the one to complain.

'I have to confess that I did something awful to him once,' Dante muttered.

Miranda tensed. Things were beginning to make sense. It sounded very much as if Guido had been hell-bent on revenge.

'What was that?' she asked gently.

'I took his girl.' Dante sighed and looked to her for understanding. 'I had no idea he was in love with her. He'd never said a word. She came on a family picnic and we got on so well that we went out together afterwards. Guido saw us—though we hadn't been trying to hide our relationship—and went berserk, yelling and sobbing and threatening me with a knife in the back. I was appalled. It was a long time before he accepted that I hadn't done it deliberately.'

'Deliberate or not,' she said soberly, 'in his eyes you still took the woman he loved.'

'I know. And I've tried to make it up to him ever since. I hope he'll meet someone special one day.'

'You're a good man,' she said shakily.

'I try. Now, enough of my brother,' he declared. 'We'll get the doctor round to check you over while Guido and I discuss business, then if the sun breaks through that cloud we can all take it easy around the pool. How does that sound?'

She managed to produce a reasonably authentic smile. 'Very idle.' And wondered how she could keep out of Guido's way for the rest of his stay.

'You should have a party,' her brother-in-law was saying, when she finally went down to the pool.

But she only had eyes for Dante. He was stretched out on a lounger, his body gleaming like polished silk. His hands were linked behind his head, lifting his chest, and when she looked at him she felt almost choked with desire.

'Excellent idea!' he replied and grinned at his brother who was sprawled on the aquamarine tiles edging the pool, one leg dangling in the water. And then Dante saw Miranda. He hurried over to her in delight and took her in his arms.

'I've missed you,' he murmured, kissing her tenderly on the mouth. 'Come and sit where I can look at you. We're planning a party. What do you think?'

She'd taken the precaution of wearing the demure one-piece. Her hair was swept to the top of her head in a no-nonsense bun, she wore no make-up and she'd wrapped a robe firmly around her body. Even so, she felt nervous as Guido's leering stare did its best to penetrate the towelling barrier.

She had the sensation that he was remembering every inch of her, and her horrified eyes saw that his hands were actually imitating caressing movements as they ran up and down his chest.

Only her immense will-power permitted her to tear her gaze from him and to answer Dante's enthusiastic response to Guido's suggestion.

'A party would be lovely,' she said coolly, sitting on the far side of Dante, well away from Guido. She had a sudden thought. It was a golden opportunity to get that test... 'I'd better go to Como town for something to wear!' she said with a little laugh.

'Women!' sighed Guido. 'Always keen to spend our money.'

Nasty, she thought. 'I was intending to spend my own,' she retorted.

'I wouldn't dream of it! Use the credit card I gave you. It needs some attention! You must buy whatever you need,' asserted Dante. 'Something special. You could ask Lizzie and your friends and people from the office to the party if you like,' he added. 'Tell me who you want to come and I'll send tickets. We'll have a fantastic party! Great idea, Guido.'

'Dancing,' Guido drawled. 'We must have an orchestra in the ballroom and perhaps a more intimate one out on the terrace so we can dance outside. What do you think, Miranda? Would you like that? To dance with your lover beneath the stars?'

Lying flat out on the sunbed, her eyes closed, her robe still firmly tied, she took a moment to deal with the nauseating thought that by 'lover' he didn't mean Dante. Why wouldn't he leave her alone? she thought miserably.

'What do you think, darling?' prompted Dante, leaning over and kissing her. His fingers busied themselves with the knot of her belt. 'Hey, are you dreaming? You must be hot like that. Here. That's better!'

'I am hot,' she said, holding back the urge to fling herself into his arms and sob her heart out in despair. 'I think I'll swim.'

'Me too!' Guido leapt up and ran to the edge of the pool, diving into the aquamarine water.

Miranda stayed put, hiding a shudder.

'Something's on your mind,' Dante said quietly.

'Yes, it is,' she mumbled.

'What?'

She bit her lip, watching Guido showing off. He interrupted his dives and handstands by energetically beckoning her to join him.

Her stomach rebelled. It was either morning sickness or she was nauseated by Guido... She didn't know. Only that she had a growing conviction that she could *never* have allowed him to get close to her. Not in *that* way, or in any way at all. She'd always kept him at arm's length. There was more to this than she'd first thought.

'My nightmares. I am trying to overcome them,' she said slowly. 'The doctor gave me some sleeping pills—though I don't want to take them. But he did say I should try to discover why I'm having recurring dreams.'

Dante's mouth had tightened. 'Miranda, I don't—'

'I know you don't want to discuss it, that it's an episode you want to forget and relegate to the past,' she said shakily, touching his arm in understanding. 'But for me it isn't over. I won't be free until I have faced my demons.'

'Even if you discover something you'd rather have kept hidden?' he muttered.

Her hand slipped away. So he wasn't sure of her innocence. He'd decided to put it behind him and hope for the best. She felt scared. If he thought she might have been unfaithful, what hope did they have for the future?

'All I want you to do,' she said, twisting the tie of her robe into a tight coil, 'is to tell me exactly what happened from your point of view. It's very important to me.' When he stayed silent, her wide blue eyes showed panic. '*Please,* Dante! You could help me.'

'Come on in!' yelled Guido.

Pained, Dante nodded curtly before turning to his brother. 'Later! Amuse yourself!' he yelled back.

'You'll do it?' she asked tremulously.

'Yes. Come on,' he muttered. 'We can't discuss this here.' His hands closed the robe over her body and he pulled her to a sitting position. 'I think we'd better go inside to discuss this.' He frowned. 'You're looking so pale and drawn that people will begin to notice,' he added as she slid her legs to the ground and rose shakily to her feet. 'You need to sleep undisturbed or your health will suffer. That won't be good for you or Carlo.'

It seemed that he was still concerned about the gossip of other people. She was so unsure of him. And would remain so, until the truth had been unravelled. As a protective measure, she withdrew into herself a little more.

'Thank you,' she said in a dull, polite tone. Because he had disappointed her. She feared that he didn't love her unconditionally—and her aching heart needed nothing less.

With a bleak expression, he collected his thin towelling robe and shrugged it on. She let him lead her off, seeing out of the corner of her eye that Guido was looking daggers at her.

Let him stew, she thought. She'd nail him, one way or the other. She had to.

Together they walked with their arms around one another, hips touching, into the house. Although she assumed this was for the benefit of anyone watching, it did feel reassuring.

His strength seemed to seep into her. If he stood by her, she could conquer all the horrors that beset her every night.

'We'll go in the library,' he said curtly, pushing open the door then locking it behind them.

In his currently detached mood she expected him to sit some distance from her, but instead he drew her down to the sofa. Enclosed by the crook of his arm, she sat rigidly, waiting for him to start. But he just stared into space, scowling, until she was prompted to urge him on.

'Dante. Please. We can't avoid this.'

'I know. I've tried, God knows, I've tried,' he said with a heavy sigh. 'It was the only way I could cope with how I felt about you.'

'Go on.'

He reached out to fiddle with an antique letter opener on the table in front of them, clearly reluctant to delve into the past. Finally he cleared his throat and she pulled in a sharp breath of relief as he began to speak.

'I'd been in Milan settling my late uncle's affairs, you remember,' he said in a low tone and she nodded. His scowl deepened, his voice grew harsher. 'I'd caught an earlier flight back than planned because I wanted to get home to see you.'

'That's nice!' she blurted out, before she could stop herself. But she was so desperate for some sign that he really cared...

'No. It's not.' Granite-faced, he shifted uncomfortably, a faint flush on his carved cheekbones. 'There'd been these rumours that you'd been neglecting Carlo while you played around with a lover—'

'You thought you'd catch me out,' she said bitterly, sinking back in deep dismay.

His mouth thinned. There was a long pause. 'Yes,' he said hoarsely. 'I had to settle my mind, to know the truth. It was crucifying me. As I was on my way home, Guido called me on my mobile—'

'*Guido?*' Suddenly she was rigid with tension, hanging on his next words.

'Yes. He said...he said I had to get back from Italy as quickly as I could—not knowing I was already in the country. He then told me that he'd called round to see you and had found you drunk on the bed—'

'Wait a minute!' she cried. Her mind whirled. 'Guido got into our apartment? How?'

'I'd given him an emergency key in case we were away and the burglar alarm went off. You need key-holders,' Dante said irritably. 'He said he'd had a hunch you were entertaining men while I was away and wanted to confront you.'

Rage bubbled up inside her. It was a good lie. 'Go on,' she said coldly.

'Unknown to him, I was only minutes away when he called,' he said in a tightly controlled voice. But she could sense his anger mounting as he relived the events of that day. 'The scene was as I have described to you before. Don't ask me to tell you again. It's branded on my brain!' he bit out with harsh resentment.

'You never mentioned that Guido was there when you arrived.'

'Just as well that he was. You weren't in a fit state to answer the door,' he slammed back.

She flinched. 'Describe him,' she demanded. 'How was he?'

'What on earth for? What difference—?'

She turned on him passionately. 'Never mind! It does make a difference! I want to know!' she cried tautly.

He gave an impatient shrug, evidently trying to remember. 'I suppose he looked shocked at what he'd discovered.'

'Why do you say that?' she shot.

'Because he looked unusually dishevelled and rather alarmed.'

'What else?'

'He was breathing hard, I remember. And he was lost for words to begin with and stammered—presumably because he was so embarrassed. I remember that he kept smoothing down his hair and pouring himself tots of whisky to steady his nerves.'

Because, she thought, cold with fury, Dante had arrived sooner than Guido had expected. Maybe…

Her heart bounded with hope. Guido had believed that Dante would arrive in England some hours later. She was sure Guido must have put something in her drink to make her pass out. Could the planned rape have been interrupted by Dante's early arrival? Was that why Guido had been so agitated? He could have heard Dante entering the apartment and gone into a flat spin, trying to get dressed before Dante reached the bedroom.

Perhaps she hadn't been violated. Her hand rested on her stomach. There might not be a pregnancy after all. She hoped so, with all her heart. If she had another baby, she wanted it to be born from love and to carry it with a heart full of dreams for the future.

'What exactly did he say?' she asked, her nerves on wires. Every cell in her brain was working overtime. Had it been a put-up job? To ruin her marriage and hurt Dante as a nasty kind of revenge? Her fists clenched as she contemplated a thousand things she'd do to Guido if he was guilty of such malice.

'He became touchingly protective of me,' Dante muttered, absently making little stabbing movements with the paper knife. 'He was very sympathetic. Urged me to save the family honour and leave at once with Carlo.' He thrust a distracted hand through his hair and dropped the knife, flinging himself back against the cushions as if collapsing beneath an impossible burden. 'I felt as if I'd been hit by a train and all my brains had been knocked out. I didn't know what to do. He advised me, stayed objective. I'll never forget what he did for me that night in organising the flight, helping to pack Carlo's toys, leaving an explanatory e-mail for you—'

'*He* wrote the e-mail?' she pounced.

'I could hardly think straight,' Dante said irritably. 'I told him what to put—'

'That…' Her voice broke. 'That I could earn my living by whoring?'

On tenterhooks, she waited for his answer. And when he jerked his head and she saw his shocked expression, her face cleared.

'I wouldn't ask him to say that!' Dante said indignantly. 'Not in a million years.'

'I have the e-mail,' she told him, her voice shaking. Now she had some proof of Guido's hatred. 'I kept it in case I had to plead my case in court. I can show it to you.'

He winced then looked down at his hands, clenched into tight fists on his knees. 'I'm sorry. Guido's doing. No doubt he was appalled by your behaviour. I just went around in a daze, filling up with caffeine while you lay on our bed...' His choked voice faded away. 'Miranda, I've had enough. I don't want to go on with this.'

He looked haunted. She felt close to tears. 'Oh, Dante! It must have been a terrible moment for you. I'm sorry to have put you through it all over again but it has helped to clarify things for me. Thank you,' she croaked.

Her hands covered her face. Guido had sent that e-mail. Not Dante. Guido had ensured that Dante had left before she had come round sufficiently to protest her innocence. He was evil personified.

'Dear heaven!' she whispered, longing to confide the truth.

Through her fingers, she looked helplessly at Dante, almost wishing he would guess. He frowned, hesitated, and then reached out for her. With a sob, she nestled up to his chest. He began to stroke her hair.

'Don't think about it,' he advised gruffly.

'But I want you to realise that someone got me drunk, perhaps spiked a soft drink with alcohol,' she said, revealing as much as she dared. 'Or they fed me a drug.'

Her hand lifted to lie against Dante's cheek and she firmly turned his granite-hard face till he was forced to look at her.

'Miranda—' he growled.

'No. Please hear me out,' she begged. 'You believe that the rumours you heard about my neglect of Carlo were untrue, don't you?'

'Yes. Except for—'

'That one time. But we've agreed something peculiar happened that evening, perhaps something beyond my control—'

'I don't understand what—'

'Dante.' She fixed him with her steady gaze. Believe me! it said. Trust me! If I was maligned unfairly over that, maybe I'm also innocent of taking a lover. And those rumours about my infidelity—whoever spread them—are lies as well.' She could see him chewing this over. Make the link! she urged silently. See what a liar your brother is! 'All I can say is that

I have never been unfaithful to you, in word, thought or deed. Whatever happened that night was not of my making.'

'But *something* happened to you! We can't pretend it didn't! I saw the aftermath!' Dante stood up, his expression wretched. '*Che Dio mi aiuti!* Excuse me,' he rasped hoarsely. 'I didn't want to do this. I didn't want to remember. I think I need to be on my own for a while. We can't keep going over and over this. It's destroying me. I think of your body and another man...' He made an angry gesture. 'You don't know what that does to me. I'm going out—'

'Where?' she cried, anxious for him.

'I don't know! Anywhere! Give my apologies to Guido.'

He was out of the room before she could rouse herself to make a protest. Miranda felt her whole body slump in despair. Dante might be prepared to believe that she hadn't deliberately invited a man into the apartment, but he thought she had been ravished, nevertheless. And he couldn't handle that.

He would be hurt beyond belief if he knew what his brother had been up to. But she couldn't bear to take no action at all.

Seething at Guido's treachery, she leapt up and prowled up and down the room, her sense of injustice getting her more and more agitated. Anger and frustration brought her to an abrupt halt. She wasn't afraid of Guido any more. He was a piece of low life, not worthy of her fear.

Chin jutting with determination, she stormed up to her room to change into something less revealing. It was time for a showdown.

In a cool white shirt and linen palazzo pants, she strode grimly to the pool, where Guido was sunning himself.

She glared down at the oil-slicked body, anger mastering the lurching disgust that this...*thing* had ever touched her.

Deliberately she picked up the jug of iced lemon and poured it all over him.

'*Dio! Che—?*'

She ignored his spluttering and grabbed his sticky hair, jerking up his head ruthlessly.

'Listen to me,' she spat, her eyes ablaze with loathing. 'I

know what you've done and what you're up to! I'm telling
you now that if you jeopardise my marriage or my access to
Carlo, I'll keep on your tail until all your lies and vile plots
are revealed! Don't mistake me, Guido! You may think I'm
calm and controlled, but where the people I love are concerned, I'm a raging tigress! And I'll have no compunction in
ripping you to shreds if you come between Dante, Carlo and
me!'

Released with a sudden contemptuous jerk of her hand, he
stared up at her. And she knew she had a terrible enemy.

'So it's war, is it?' he said nastily. 'I wonder who will win?
I can bring you down just like *that*.' He snapped his fingers.

'Rubbish,' she said with cold hauteur.

And before he noticed that she was shaking like a leaf, she
walked swiftly away.

Open hostilities had been declared. She took a deep breath
and let it out slowly. She had better watch her back. And get
to Como town for that test as soon as possible.

CHAPTER ELEVEN

To HER dismay, Dante decided to accompany her on the long drive to Como.

'But surely you don't want to come shopping with me!' she protested over breakfast.

He didn't look at her but concentrated on buttering his croissant.

'I want to introduce you to my staff in my silk mills there,' he said with a firmness that didn't brook argument. 'They've been asking to meet you. I think it would be rude not to call in.'

He was frowning. His white teeth took a bite from the pastry and he busied himself with catching stray flakes with his forefinger, which he then licked clean before wiping it on a napkin and helping Carlo to scoop up the last of his strawberries.

She watched Dante sadly. They had made love the previous night. But it had been different. Less tender, more…desperate.

She felt as if she was on a tightrope and might fall off any minute. Guido might persuade Dante that she wasn't worth persevering with.

'I would like to meet everyone very much,' she said, evenly, hoping to find a moment to herself when she could slip into a pharmacy.

The more people she met, she reckoned, the more likely it was that Dante would realise that other people could see she was a straightforward kind of person who wouldn't lie easily.

She leaned forward and lightly touched his hand. He jumped and hastily reclaimed it. Hurt by his rejection, she gritted her teeth and tried not to panic.

'I want to meet all your friends. And I want you to meet

mine again. You liked them, didn't you? Some have known
me ever since we were at school together.'

For a moment his glance flicked up. 'They're very fond of
you, I remember,' he conceded curtly.

And just as she was going to point out that there might be
a reason her friends had been loyal to her for so long, Carlo
claimed their time.

Not long after that they set off for Como. She deliberately
kept her conversation light and minimal on the drive down the
eastern side of the lake.

Dante seemed disinclined to do much more than offer
monosyllabic answers to her questions about the places they
passed, though he pulled out all the stops when they reached
the silk mill.

Before she had time to dwell on the fear that he might be
back to keeping up appearances, she was enfolded in a warm
welcome by his staff and whisked off on a tour which was
conducted with such pride and evident affection that she was
caught up in everyone's enthusiasm.

'And,' the sales manager told her with excited gestures as
he turned the pages of sample books showing international
models in Severini silk creations, 'as I'm sure you know, we
sell our silk to the fashion houses of Europe. See. Here…'

'Wonderful!' she exclaimed in admiration. 'It's an impres-
sive record. Signor Gordati,' she said hesitantly, aware that
Dante was on the telephone in another office, 'you haven't
found it hard, changing from having *Il Conte* Amadeo Severini
as your boss, and adapting to the ways of my husband?'

She felt bad, asking. Yet she needed confirmation that Dante
was essentially good-hearted. Guido's lies had left a legacy of
doubts.

The sales manager beamed at her. 'Hard?' he exclaimed.
'We are delighted. Amadeo was remarkable. A father to us
all. And we are fortunate indeed that your husband we have
known for many years and he is loved as our brother.'

She smiled, happy to know that. 'And Guido?' she asked
gently.

Signor Gordati's brows drew together in a ferocious frown. 'Perhaps, *Contessa*,' he said with dignity, 'we should be thinking of lunch?'

That was a deliberate evasion. She nodded slowly, reading the man's anxious eyes.

'You are loyal and tactful,' she murmured.

He kissed her hand. 'And I am honoured to meet you, *Contessa*.'

She looked up as Dante appeared in the doorway, his eyes thoughtful as he studied her and his manager.

'They were impressed with you,' Dante said abruptly when they were walking from a car park to the cathedral square. 'You asked interesting questions. Thank you.'

'I *was* interested. It's a fascinating business.'

Unbend, she pleaded silently. But he remained formal and polite all through lunch. And he insisted on taking her around the boutiques afterwards, helping her to choose party clothes. As a result, she had no opportunity to slip away.

It was late when they drove back along the western arm of the lake. The views were wonderful, the villages elegant and colourful with flowers, but all she felt was frustration.

Even the evening light on the mountains failed to enchant her. The mountains glowed pinkly above a grey silk lake. Slowly the sky darkened, the line of the jagged peaks becoming hard and forbidding against the paler night sky.

It echoed Dante's behaviour. He had changed. Part of her wished they hadn't talked through the events of that fateful night when he'd walked out on her. Ever since, he had been horribly uncommunicative and distant. Even to the extent of avoiding her.

As the days went by, he became more and more withdrawn. Except in bed. They still slept together, and made love, though even that was fierce and frantic with none of the deep affection that had sent her into ecstasies.

In the mornings he seemed consumed by anger. He wouldn't look at her, nor did he attempt to comfort her whenever she woke from the nightmare. And she didn't know what to do, other than to wait it out and keep her own feelings under wraps.

If he was going to reject her then she knew she had to start shutting down her emotions. She didn't want to. But she didn't want to be hurt, either. She had to survive.

If they were to live like this, using one another for sex and pretending to be happily married, then she had to take steps to protect herself.

'Dante not around?'

It was late evening and Carlo was still up. In the middle of reading a story to him, she glanced up briefly at Guido, who'd come into the drawing room, and replied with a curt, 'Working.'

He laughed as if he harboured a secret. Sickened, she watched the hated face come close to hers. His finger reached out to tickle Carlo, who squealed and clung to her tightly.

To her horror she saw Guido's finger slide boldly into her deep cleavage with the clear intent of curving beneath her breast. She gagged, and it was a moment before she could clamp her hand on his wrist and pull away.

And by then he was looking towards the door—where Dante stood as if turned to stone. Miranda went scarlet at the ferocity of her husband's inky black glare. He spun abruptly on his heel and left without a word.

If she hadn't been cuddling her son, she would have slapped Guido's triumphant face. But she could do nothing.

'*Get out!*' she grated under her breath, disgusted by what had happened.

'Why don't we come to a nice little arrangement—?'

'You Severinis and your arrangements!' she hissed. 'You're ruining my marriage—'

'I think I've probably exceeded my welcome too.' Guido grinned. 'I must make my move quickly, before I'm asked to leave.'

'What do you mean?'

'You'll see.'

White-faced, she stared after his swaggering figure. The

door shut very softly and she cuddled Carlo very hard, much to his delight.

Her mind whirled. Since he'd arrived, Guido had constantly tried to paw her, jumping away from her with theatrical guilt whenever Dante came near. She knew what he was doing. Sowing more doubts. And succeeding, by the look of it.

After she'd put her son to bed, she sought out Dante and found him outside on the terrace, staring at the crescent moon. The sky was a dense black and spattered with stars. Cassiopeia, the Plough, the Milky Way. Timeless wonders.

Before she could attract his attention he began to walk through the garden, and she caught up the material of her billowing taffeta skirt and followed till he reached the little temple by the lakeside and leaned against one of its elegant pillars.

It was very quiet. Warm lights glowed in the blackness, marking the villages across the lake, their reflections shimmering in the patent-leather water.

Something caught in her heart. It was all so beautiful. Especially Dante. The pale gleam from one of the lamps strung along their shoreline was highlighting the carved contours of his face.

'Dante,' she said, helplessly soft and loving despite her intentions.

He started. 'I came here to be alone,' he growled.

She wouldn't be put off. This was too important.

'And I came after you to make a request.' She moved closer, wishing he wasn't so hard and unyielding. 'Send Guido away,' she pleaded. 'He's pestering me and I don't like it.'

He shot her a cold glance. 'That's not how it looks from where I stand.'

Miranda frowned. Absently slid up a rogue bootlace strap of her low-cut turquoise top and quailed at Dante's glare of contempt. She knew that he was remembering his brother's questing finger. But why was he angry with her?

'You think I encouraged him,' she said jerkily.

The coal-black eyes blazed. 'He explained to me just now,'

he snapped. 'He was tickling Carlo and you grabbed his hand—'

'*No!*' she cried in horror. 'It wasn't like that! I was *stopping* him—'

'*Basta!*' He abruptly turned his back on her. She could see that he was shaking with anger. 'He's been complaining about you ever since he arrived. You…' There was a pause. The atmosphere was electric with tension and Miranda couldn't speak for misery, emotion filling her throat with a hard, hurting pain. 'I want you to move back into your own room,' he clipped.

She drew in a steadying breath and forced herself to croak out,

'Why, Dante?'

The look he threw her over his shoulder was so filled with anguish and loathing that she gave a cry of alarm and stumbled back, almost falling over her full skirts.

'So you do know my name!' he scathed.

Her hand went to her heaving breast. 'What are you talking about?'

Slowly he came to face her, his eyes glittering. 'Very tragic. Very beautiful. You even look vulnerable and innocent. A few days ago I would have slowly and lovingly ravished you if you'd posed like that for me.'

She swallowed. There was no longer any affection or desire in him. Just a boiling rage. Guido had poisoned him against her.

'But not now,' she said in a low tone.

'No. Not when you murmur my brother's name in your sleep,' he snarled savagely, and with an expression of utter hatred he strode away.

'Oh, God!' she whispered, rooted to the spot.

She had condemned herself, out of her own lips! She closed her eyes and battled for control over the overwhelming urge to fling herself on the grass and cry till she could weep no more. But she couldn't. She choked back the tears, biting her lip till it drew blood. She had to pull herself together. Now.

Her sister and her friends were arriving any minute for the party the next night and she had to behave as though nothing had happened, even though her world had fallen apart.

This was Guido's revenge. To make Dante believe that she'd been flirting with his own brother.

'Damn you, Guido!' she seethed, dashing away the hot tears which had escaped from her burning eyes.

He was clever, she'd give him that. If she ever decided to tell Dante that it must have been Guido who'd laced her drink, then he'd think she was making excuses—and that she'd been perfectly willing.

Miranda groaned. Slowly she began to trudge back. She reflected unhappily that Dante would never give her the benefit of the doubt if she did announce that she was pregnant. He'd be convinced it was Guido's child. And the horror of it was that he could be right.

Dante didn't trust her. He believed the worst. She came to a halt and covered her face with her hands in utter despair.

'Oh, when will I know if I'm pregnant?' she moaned.

There would be no time the next day for a trip to Como. The hours would be taken up with entertaining Lizzie and her friends.

With her eyes awash in unshed tears, she studied the elegant façade of the *palazzo*. Everyone would think she'd landed on her feet. A gorgeous husband, an adorable child and a fairy-tale palace full of beautiful antiques and glorious paintings.

They'd admire the Venetian glasses, the frescoed walls and ceilings and the hand-carved oak staircase. At night they'd slip into the bed linen of sand-washed silk with the Severini orchid embroidered on the edges, and they would envy her.

But all those riches, together with the lemon-tree walk, the stream and waterfalls, the orchard and the stunning views, were nothing without Dante's love and trust. She would swap them all for that. For an end to this torment. The loneliness.

All she wanted was to be loved. Was that too much to hope for?

*   *   *

'Lizzie!'

She stared, aghast, at the scene before her eyes. She had to say something. Couldn't let her sister be fooled… Ever since she'd arrived the previous night, Lizzie had been glued to Guido.

It was the afternoon of the party now, and everyone was taking a rest. But she and Dante were checking the arrangements.

In supervising the placing of strings of lights down to the river, she'd been horrified to see her sister and Guido in a passionate embrace.

'Lizzie!' she called, more desperately.

Her sister saw her, gave the grinning Guido a little push and ran happily to her side. 'Isn't this all fantastic? I'm so happy for you. Now. What do you want, darling?' she prattled, her eyes alight with excitement.

'My dress!' Miranda lied, raising her voice, not wanting to alert Guido to the real reason she was taking Lizzie away. 'I need your input. One is very glam and glittery, the other's grand and simple…'

'Say no more.' Lizzie tucked her arm in Miranda's and began to walk back with her. 'You must be a bag of nerves, all these important—'

'Liz! I have to tell you something,' Miranda whispered on impulse. 'You won't like it.'

'You look horribly pale!' Lizzie said in concern. 'You're in trouble—'

'Wait till we're in my room,' Miranda replied in agitation, longing to unload some of her burden. 'I've so much to say.'

Unusually, Lizzie listened without interruption, such was the shock of Miranda's story as the words tumbled out—the whole story, from beginning to end.

Miranda was sobbing when she'd finished. 'I know you won't believe me,' she jerked. 'You're crazy about Guido and—'

'Darling Miranda!' Unusually sombre, Lizzie wrapped her

arms around her elder sister. 'He's good-looking and he's loaded and we've had a kiss or two, but I was never crazy about him. And the more I got to know him, the less I liked him. I'm so sorry this has happened to you. I'm appalled at what you've gone through. If only you'd confided in me! I love and admire you more than any woman I know. If you say this is true, then it is. You don't tell lies, I know that.'

'I wish Dante was as loyal as you,' Miranda sighed.

'Darling, he's horribly jealous. And be fair, it must have looked as if he'd caught you after one hell of an orgy. Even worse, you've been calling out his brother's name in your sleep. It would take a saint not to doubt you—and he's a hot-blooded Italian with a passionate nature. He's struggling to make sense of what happened. And I'm sure he's trying hard to accept it. Things'll turn out OK in the end. Honest. Dante loves you to pieces.'

'Don't give me false hope. You're only saying that—' Miranda mumbled.

'No. He does. Believe me. He can't keep his eyes or his hands off you, Miranda. I saw how he looked at you last night. He wants to believe you, but I bet he can't get that scene out of his head.'

Miranda shuddered. 'Neither can I! And I don't know what to do!'

'You've got to tell him why Guido figures in your dreams,' Lizzie said firmly.

'I don't know that I can! He adores his brother—'

'Are you mad?' Lizzie gave her an impatient little shake. 'He's a rat. First you, then he has a go at me! How dare he? The little squirt doesn't deserve your silence! You've got into the habit of keeping your mouth shut over the years. This is the time to speak out—'

'Not yet,' Miranda said, her face wan. 'We're both too emotional, too upset. Perhaps when Guido's gone…' Her words tailed away. She couldn't bear for Dante to think so badly of her.

Lizzie gave her a consoling hug. 'Don't lose heart now. You love him too much to give up. And he'll come round in time.'

Miranda shuddered. 'And if I *am* pregnant?' she wailed.

'Very unlikely,' Lizzie declared stoutly. 'I'll get that test for you in Bellagio today—I'll go out now. I've got to get some stuff from the chemist anyway. I've had an infection in my ear and I'm on antibiotics for a couple more days.' She made a face. 'That means no booze for a while! Oh, and Guido says he's leaving for London after the party, so you and Dante will have time alone together to work on your marriage.'

Astonished by Lizzie's supportive attitude, Miranda dashed her hand across her eyes and gave a shaky little smile.

'Thank you. You've held me together,' she whispered.

Her sister hugged her again. 'Thank *you*. For all the sacrifices. I owe you my entire childhood, my untroubled life. Now you're in trouble, I'll do anything I can to make things right again.'

The two sisters embraced, a deeper understanding and warmth existing between them. Odd, Miranda mused, how something good always came from something bad.

'I must go. I've got to check everything's OK for the party,' she said with a rueful smile.

'Good thing. Take your mind off it all,' Lizzie encouraged. 'Scoot!'

Tense and on edge but determined to stay optimistic, Miranda managed to liaise with Dante over a couple of problems connected with the catering, and then they threw themselves into some energetic games with Carlo.

By the time he'd been tucked up in bed, she felt exhausted. Ahead lay a night of bright chatter and play-acting. Steeling herself, she selected the beautiful sapphire dress she and Dante had chosen, and let it slither down over her naked body.

It shimmered with every movement, cradling her breasts and pushing them up in a subtle invitation. She turned around to see the back. Or, rather, her back, since the dress dipped in a figure-hugging curve to her waist. It was daring. But Dante had loved it and it made her feel a million dollars.

Carefully she applied her make-up and swept her hair to the top of her head, taking pains to ensure the overall effect was both elegant and sexy.

Slipping her feet into a pair of sensationally high sandals, she walked into Dante's quarters, her entire body trembling with nervous strain and hope.

He had to fall in love with her all over again. If he looked into her eyes he'd see his name written there. If he had any sensitivity at all he'd feel the passion flowing from every part of her.

He was staring out of the window and wearing a tuxedo, which had clearly been built around his body by a talented tailor. For a moment or two she devoured him hungrily with her eyes, then said with deceptive coolness,

'Will I do?'

With apparent reluctance, he turned to face her. She noticed his jaw tightening, a convulsive swallow. But nothing else in his expression told her that he found her desirable.

'Perfect,' he said shortly, as if she were an item in a shop window. 'But not that silver chain.'

A little puzzled, she fingered the necklace and watched him open a safe. He brought a box to her and opened it. She gasped.

'Dante!'

'My uncle's mother owned them. Put them on.'

Awed, she took the dainty flower-shaped sapphire and diamond earrings from the box and fixed them to her lobes. The diamond necklace looked fragile, fashioned as a scattering of interlaced flowers, each centre a perfect sapphire.

'It's absolutely beautiful!' she breathed.

He watched her struggling to fasten it. After a moment, and with a mutter of irritation, Dante came behind Miranda to do it for her.

His fingers were cool on her hot skin. Tingles of electricity flew across her skin from wherever he touched.

Hardly breathing, she looked over at their reflection in the huge baroque mirror decorated with golden cherubs, and felt a pang of love for the dark-haired man who hovered so enticingly close.

'Dante,' she murmured.

'Time we went down,' he said sharply, moving away. 'Miranda…'

Her voice lifted with hope. 'Yes?'

My darling, she added in her mind.

He exhaled sharply. 'We must be affectionate in public,' he rasped. She nodded, disappointed. 'But don't imagine,' he growled, 'for one second, that I mean anything I do or say.'

Stoically she took the blow and hid the fact that she reeled from it. 'I'm sorry you don't trust me,' she said quietly.

'How can I,' he hurled, 'after the things I've seen and heard?'

Good will triumph, she told herself. And with dignity, said, 'Shall we go?'

'It means nothing to you, does it?' he snarled. 'Our marriage is destroyed, our child's happiness is threatened and you have condemned me to living with a cheating, lying harlot—'

'Our guests will be arriving,' she reminded him, controlling her shaking hands. The pain was making her feel faint. 'We must be there to meet them.'

This wasn't the moment to fight her corner. She was too close to tears, and she didn't want to let him down by appearing before his friends with her wounded heart on view.

'Of course.'

Abruptly Dante jerked out his arm and she slipped her hand into it, her fingers resting on the sensually soft material.

'I love you,' she insisted. He glanced at her, his eyes tarry black and on fire with contempt and anger. She felt his hurt and wanted to ease it. Tenderly she persevered, 'One day you will know that is true. I hope it will be soon because my heart is breaking—' She had gone too far. Her eyes were blurred with tears. Hastily she averted her gaze and wished she'd kept her own counsel. 'Let's go,' she husked.

And as they moved towards the sound of music, she wondered how she would find the strength to endure the next five or six hours.

CHAPTER TWELVE

IT WAS the friendliness and affection of their guests that buoyed her up. Dazed by their compliments, touched by their goodwill towards her, she was surprised to find she was enjoying herself.

Until the first dance.

She was talking to Felipe and some of Dante's business friends when she saw Dante crossing the ballroom floor. His gaze was fixed on her: dark, compelling and so intensely sexy that it made a *frisson* run through her.

Miranda felt an irresistible force pulling her towards him. He held out his hand.

'My regrets, gentlemen, but I have come to take my wife away from you. We are to start the dancing,' he said in an oddly husky voice.

Dumbly she reached out trembling fingers and found them clasped in his warm grip. And then she was in his arms, the music swelling and swirling all around her as he swept her into a series of spins that left her elated and dizzy.

'You must talk to me,' he rasped, his eyes blazing at her from under his brows. It seemed to her that he wanted to be anywhere but here, with her in his arms.

She licked her lips and said the first thing that came into her head. 'I love dancing with you.'

As if weakened by this confession, she sank, boneless, deeper into his arms. Somehow her head was on his shoulder. The warmth of his hand, splaying over her naked spine, penetrated deeply. Miranda surrendered herself to him, her fingers pressed firmly against his frantically beating heart.

And then his body shifted and she drew in a sharp breath of desire.

'Yes,' he muttered. 'I can't hide the fact that I want you. I curse the day you were born! Any man would desire you, the way you look tonight. You're temptation itself. The archetypal ice queen challenging man's ability to melt that veneer of reserve and tap the heat beneath.'

Again he was making her feel like an object to be possessed rather than a woman with feelings. 'I don't want just sex with you,' she protested.

'It'll have to do. I'm giving nothing more.' He nuzzled her ear and she whimpered, loving it. 'You're killing me slowly, you know that?' he muttered harshly. 'Every time I touch you—and I find that I must—I think of another man, another time. I think of him holding you, kissing you, hearing you cry out...*knowing* you.'

'Oh, Dante! I'm sorry,' she mumbled, but he'd buried his face in her neck and was grinding out broken sentences in anguished Italian.

Cold air hit the warm skin of her back. Pulling away, she saw they were on the terrace outside. Dante's entire body tensed and at first she thought it was the shock of the fresh air. But when she followed his glittering gaze she saw that he was staring down at Guido in the garden below.

Miranda's hand flew to her mouth. Lizzie was in Guido's arms and he was forcing her backwards while she struggled to avoid his marauding mouth.

Suddenly, before either Miranda or Dante could collect their wits, Lizzie freed a hand and brought it across Guido's face with a resounding crack.

Hastily released, Lizzie said something obviously terse and to the point, and picking up the skirts of her dress, she stomped up the wide steps to the ballroom terrace.

'Lizzie! Darling!' Concerned, Miranda ran to her sister. 'Are you all right?'

Lizzie nodded. Guido glared up at them all, his eyes so murderous that Miranda felt a chill freezing the bones of her spine. He strode angrily into the house through the library door.

below and she turned to her sister, who was checking her pinkened arm where Guido had grasped it.

'I feel fine for giving him a slap!' Lizzie declared. 'And,' she said, turning to the grim-faced Dante, 'don't think I was leading your brother on. I can see you're inclined to blame me for that scene. Well, it's about time you talked to a few people about your brother and asked them their honest opinion—'

'Lizzie, please—!' Miranda began nervously, fearing where this might lead.

'No. This needs saying,' her feisty sister retorted. 'Ask the women in the office where he works, Dante. Ask the men there, too. He's a groper. And a liar. Stop protecting your little brother and start seeing the truth for once. Ask yourself who you should trust. Your wife or your brother. Listen to your instincts, you idiot!'

Dante felt a shock run through him as though he'd been slapped too. It was true that he'd been appalled to see his brother handling Lizzie so roughly. Suddenly he recalled the many accusations from women that Guido had dated.

And for the first time, although he'd previously dismissed the idea as ridiculous, he began to wonder if it had been Guido who'd plied Miranda with drink that fateful night. His brother had clearly been in a panic...and he'd looked so guilty...

But he felt sure that Guido couldn't have poured alcohol down Miranda's throat unless she'd been willing. And she'd been stupid to sit in her bedroom and consume an entire litre of champagne. It was obvious what would happen next.

He clenched his jaw and pressed his hand to his forehead, trying not to pursue that thought. But images of Miranda, writhing luxuriously beneath his brother, kept intruding on his mind. It would explain the strange tensions between the two of them. And why she called out Guido's name in the night.

He felt as though someone were slashing at his guts with knives. And couldn't bear it much more. He felt as if he had been personally violated.

He stifled a groan. She claimed she loved him. But Guido

insisted she was only saying that because he was the one with the title and the wealth. Dante felt the doubts pile into his mind. He had thought there was love in her eyes, but maybe he was fooling himself. Plenty of men were led a dance by clever women.

He couldn't blame her. She'd had a dog's life. Why shouldn't she want a wealthy man to look after her for a change?

Maybe it was his fault that he had neglected Miranda in those days when he was visiting his dying uncle. He'd been exhausted keeping the business running and giving his uncle all his spare time.

During that period she'd been distant and more reserved than ever with him. Guido had explained why. That she'd been seeing other men behind his back. One of them being Guido, it seemed.

Dante gritted his teeth. At that time, his emotions had been strained to their limits by his beloved uncle's failing health and he couldn't handle the prospect of being hurt by her. So he'd kept his head and had been polite and cool in return.

Possibly, he mused, his brother had been preparing him for the fact that the 'other man' she'd fallen for was actually Guido himself...

'Dante!' Lizzie glared at him and gave his arm a little shake. He stared down at her, dazed. 'What's the matter?' she demanded. 'You've got to open your eyes and see what a lying little randy runt your brother is! I won't stand by and see my sister's life ruined by a jealous louse! She sacrificed her childhood for me,' she went on vehemently. 'She's unselfish and loving and deserves better from you! All her life she's had to hide her feelings and I've tried and tried to make her trust us with her emotions. You're ruining everything. You're forcing her to crawl back into her shell because she's so scared of loving you too much and being rejected!'

Dante blinked, startled by Lizzie's outburst. She was loyal and he admired her for that. But he still couldn't forget the

Technicolor pictures of Miranda and her lover that filled his head every waking minute. Torturing him.

Despairing of a solution to the situation, he looked into Lizzie's bright, intense eyes and flushed face. And frowned at what he saw.

'Are you drunk?' he asked suspiciously.

'I wish!' Lizzie gave a rueful sigh.

Miranda's arm went around her sister. 'Lizzie's been on orange juice all night. She's on antibiotics,' she explained quietly. 'The sparkle is entirely due to sisterly indignation.'

His gaze swivelled to Miranda and his breath caught at her ethereal beauty. Something inside him snapped.

This couldn't go on. He'd deal with this now. Confront his brother. Hear a blow-by-blow account of what had happened that night and get Guido to explain his strange manner. Then... He jammed his teeth together. Then it would be Miranda's turn. He had to know why she moaned Guido's name every damn night.

Without a word, he turned abruptly on his heel and went hunting.

Miranda watched him leave, her heart heavy. 'Thanks for your support,' she mumbled. 'He won't listen to the truth. I don't know what to do. This is all such a mess.'

Lizzie patted her shoulder. 'He'll come round in time. I'm ashamed to say I enjoyed dealing with Guido. That slap was as much for you as it was for me. Oh! I almost forgot!' she cried. 'I've got the test here!' She looked around, found they were unobserved, and slipped it from her bag.

Miranda gulped. 'I—I c-can't do it!' she cried in panic.

'You can. You will. I'll come with you. Is there a quick way to your room?'

Miranda nodded dumbly, her throat dry with nerves. Prodded into action by Lizzie, she led her sister around the back of the house and up the servants' stairs.

'I'm so scared!' she admitted, when they'd reached her suite of rooms.

'Come on, toughie. Do it. For your peace of mind.' Lizzie

gave her a hug and pushed her into the bathroom. 'And get a move on!' she yelled as the door closed.

She forced herself to read the instructions. Then made herself go through with the test. And waited an eternity for the result.

Everything hinged on this. Her future with Dante and Carlo. Her happiness. She couldn't bear to look. Kept her eyes tightly shut. Begged the fates to make it negative. Only then could she build the love between herself and Dante. Only then…

She glanced quickly down. Her eyes rounded in horror.

Positive!

Lizzie's eyes were round with sympathetic dismay. 'What are you going to do?' she asked.

'What I always do,' Miranda answered. 'Cope.'

Dante searched everywhere, fuming when it seemed his brother had vanished into thin air. For half an hour he neglected his guests to no avail. The showdown would have to wait—but he'd hunt him down, he thought grimly, wherever he was. There'd be no escaping this confrontation.

Tense and edgy with frustration, he returned to mingle with his guests, exchanging pleasantries and trying to behave as though nothing had happened to blight his life.

'Dante! I must compliment you. Your wife is stunning, the talk of Bellagio,' murmured a voice by his elbow.

'I think so too,' he replied politely, not even registering who it was.

Following the gesturing hand, he then saw Miranda descending the grand staircase. His heart turned over as it always did. If only, he thought, jagged pains tearing through his body.

Vaguely he saw that Lizzie, dazzling in her scarlet and orange ball gown, was following Miranda, but he wasn't interested in her. It was his wife who held his gaze as she glided like a swan through into the ballroom.

There was something extraordinary about her—as if she was in a world of her own: remote, detached, almost luminously pale. Among the five hundred people in glittering array, she stood out like a beacon of light. Slender, curvy, unbelievably sexy and yet oddly untouchable and fragile. He devoured her, everything about her.

The carriage of her body seemed more regal than usual, he thought. She was the colour of marble, but with high spots of colour on her cheeks. And so beautiful. His mouth tightened.

Someone spoke to her. A young man, evidently smitten. She remained charming but aloof to his flattery.

Dante tried not to be obsessed by her. With an effort, he responded courteously to the conversation of several people who'd drifted up to him and they teased him because his gaze continually strayed to Miranda.

Because there *was* something other-worldly about her. And it intrigued and touched him more than he could ever have imagined.

'Yes,' he found himself saying fervently. 'I am fortunate. I love her with all my heart.' And he knew that this was true. The knowledge rocked him.

'I've noticed how she seeks you out all the time,' someone murmured.

Across the room, his eyes met Miranda's troubled gaze. He felt his body burst into life. The pain ebbed away. He tried a smile and she visibly quivered, her hand going to her mouth, her lovely eyes fixed mesmerically on his as if in a wordless plea of half-fearful hope.

It seemed that love flooded the entire room, filling his head with a dizzy sensation. It came to him then in a blinding flash. What had happened didn't matter. He loved her and he had to trust her when she said she felt the same. He would concentrate on the way they felt now. Heal the marriage. His love was strong enough to overcome anything.

His expression became radiant as he turned to his gently amused—and envious—guests.

'*Permesso…*' he husked. 'I'm going to tell her so, right now, if you'll excuse me.'

Behind him, women sighed and men cleared their throats as he made his way a little unsteadily through the dancing couples towards her. She seemed to be waiting, with a bright-ness in her eyes that might have been tears or it might have been joy. He would find out, he thought happily.

And then, briefly diverted by an old family friend, he caught a glimpse of Guido, stealthily skirting the room as if looking for someone. He was torn, wanting to confront his brother, yet also longing to tell Miranda how he felt. Glancing back at Miranda, he saw that she was now surrounded by a group of people and hidden from sight.

He'd see Guido first. It would only take a moment and it was of the utmost importance. He and Miranda had all the time in the world to love one another. He would catch up with her in the garden and… He smiled. He would shower her with kisses. Beg her forgiveness. Tell her how much he loved her.

Detaching himself from his friend with practised expertise, he headed for his brother, who was standing to the left of a broad pillar—as if in hiding.

He frowned, then froze in his tracks as he watched Guido slip something from his pocket. Reaching around the pillar, Guido emptied a powder into a glass of orange juice which had been placed on a small table.

A woman's hand picked up the glass. Although he couldn't see who it was because of the pillar, there was no mistaking the bright scarlet and orange skirts pooling on the floor. Dante let out a hiss of hot breath. Guido had spiked Lizzie's drink. Terror gripped him as everything began to slot into place. He knew what was happening. Didn't want to acknowledge it, but the evidence was screaming at him.

In a state of shock he began to move towards his sister-in-law. The empty glass was set down on the table and he wanted to yell in despair but managed to restrain himself. This was too shameful to become public. To his frustration, it was im-possible to make much progress because the floor was packed and everyone wanted to speak to him.

His brain whirled with a thousand thoughts clamouring to be heard. Truth upon sickening truth crashed into his mind as he tried to reach the unsuspecting Lizzie.

'Dante! You look dreadful! What is it?'

He whirled at Miranda's gentle query.

'It's Lizzie,' he said tersely. 'I think she's in terrible trouble.'

Alarm flashed in Miranda's eyes when she followed Dante's gaze and saw her sister lurch into Guido's waiting arms.

'I don't understand! She can't be drunk!' she cried, as she and Dante battled through the throng.

'Drugged, I think,' Dante gritted, fuming as his brother looped Lizzie's arm around his neck and proceeded to drag her out of the room.

Miranda gasped, her face white when she looked at him. 'Dante! Not…?'

'I fear so,' he replied shakily, the horror of his brother's wickedness bleaching his taut skin.

Free of the crowd at last, he and Miranda began to run. He pulled out his mobile and called for an ambulance.

'Guido!' Miranda yelled and was startled by Guido's fury when he jerked his head around and saw them as they caught up with him in the hallway.

'It's all right, I'll deal with her,' Guido said quickly. 'She's drunk. I'll take her up to her room. Go back to your guests. OK, Liz?'

Lizzie's flushed face lifted to Guido's. Her eyes were unfocused. 'Okey dokey,' she said in a slow, slurred voice. Her legs collapsed beneath her.

'How much have you knocked back?' marvelled Guido. 'What a little tramp! Doesn't she know it's not done to get drunk in public in this country?'

Dante swallowed hard. So glib. He couldn't bear it. The lies slid off his brother's tongue with appalling ease! It felt as if a steel clamp had crushed his chest. All his hopes for Guido, his love and loyalty and devotion, had been turned to ashes in his mouth.

'She's not drunk,' he snarled. 'She's been ill. And she's been on soft drinks all evening because she's taking antibiotics. I've sent for an ambulance. For the moment, we'll take her into the library.'

Alarm spread over Guido's face but Dante's superior strength and inner fury left Guido no option but to obey.

'She is drunk!' his brother protested, once the door had been kicked shut by Dante's foot. 'Cancel the ambulance—think of the publicity, the gossip! Look, leave me with her. I'll keep a watch.'

Dante could hardly contain himself. But he kept silent until they had slid the unconscious Lizzie onto the sofa. And then he walked up to his brother. Before Guido knew what he was doing, he had thrust his hand into Guido's pocket and extracted a vial.

As he read the label his breath hissed in. Black and storm-laden, his contemptuous gaze fixed on the cringing Guido.

'I was right. You disgusting little pervert! This is a rape drug, isn't it?' he snarled as Guido moved back, whimpering denials. Nausea hit Dante's stomach and he moved menacingly towards his terrified brother.

The room whirled as Dante's words sank in. For a moment Miranda swayed, then she recovered, kneeling beside her sister and anxiously checking her pulse.

'Are you all right? Can you look after Lizzie?' Dante asked her grimly. 'I have something I must do.'

'I'm fine. I can cope,' she said, ignoring the chaotic thoughts in her head. This was exactly what must have happened to her. Sickened, she clenched her jaw then forced herself to stay calm for Lizzie's sake. 'You deal with Guido. Get him out of our sight.'

As Miranda soothed her sister, Dante began to interrogate Guido in fast, biting Italian. She flicked a glance at his white face, his eyes burning black, his mouth a thin slit of fury as Guido replied. Unable to understand what was being said, she concentrated on Lizzie.

'Women aren't safe with you around!' she heard Dante snarl.

'It was a one-off!' Guido protested desperately. 'Two women who adored you—'

'And all the others you've treated roughly over the years? What if another woman rejects you—will you take what you want and to hell with her? You know I can't let this go. Dear God, Guido, have you any idea what you've done? What hell you've put us through? Miranda's life is ruined. Mine. Carlo's. Our marriage cracked. You are my brother, my flesh and blood, and I'm responsible for you but, by God, I won't shirk from what I must do. Come with me. You've gone too far for this to be brushed under the carpet.'

Miranda shook at Dante's grief. After a scuffle, Dante caught Guido's arm in a lock behind his back. Ignoring his brother's panic-stricken pleading, he drove Guido out of the room.

Trembling, she stroked Lizzie's pale face, whispering comforting words to her. And she felt cold as ice inside because Dante had said quite clearly that their marriage was broken asunder. She fought back the tears and tried to think of Lizzie's needs. After a while the door snapped open again and she jumped at the sound of Dante's heavy tread. He came to kneel beside her.

'Where's Guido?' she asked sharply.

'With Luca and the gardener,' Dante replied, his tone tightly controlled. 'I've called the police. I want him put behind bars.'

Miranda's eyes rounded. 'Dante—!'

Sickly he shook his head as if he didn't want to face what he'd done. 'Lizzie—how is she?' he growled.

Her heart went out to him but she knew he wanted time to get over the dreadful shame and humiliation of discovering the truth about his brother. Gently she said,

'Her pulse is better than it was. I'll be glad when the ambulance comes, though. It's OK, sweetheart,' she said softly to her sister. 'I'm here—'

'She can't hear you,' Dante rasped. 'Can't you see, she's unconscious?'

The nightmare flashed into her head. She remembered how it had been for her. And she lifted her strained face to his.

'You're wrong! She *can* hear me! Every word!' she cried jerkily. 'I know! I remember!'

'Yes,' he muttered. 'I believe you do. Guido...' His voice broke. 'I made him admit that he spiked your drink too. I know nothing that happened was your fault.'

Tears filled her eyes but she blinked them away. Dante knew everything now and, although he'd realise that she hadn't invited Guido's attentions, nothing else had changed. It hadn't altered the fact that she had been defiled. And was carrying a rapist's child. Her misery was overwhelming. She shrugged as if nothing mattered any more.

'Miranda—' he choked.

She put out her hand to stop him from saying anything. She could only deal with one crisis at a time.

'Not now. My sister needs me,' she muttered. 'Lizzie,' she said lovingly, 'you'll be fine. A headache, some nausea. But you'll have no bad memories, because you are safe. I'm here with you. Go to sleep. Hush. Sleep...'

When they returned from the hospital, reassured that Lizzie was asleep and would be well cared for, it seemed incongruous—and almost an insult—that the party was still in full swing.

'Oh, no!' Miranda groaned. 'I can't face anyone.'

'You don't have to,' Dante clipped, his face hard as granite.

They'd hardly spoken to one another for the past two hours. Not touching, as separate as two strangers who'd never met, they slowly climbed the stairs. Miranda felt her heart was breaking. This could be her last night in the villa. Maybe Dante would let her live near by so that she could see Carlo—

'I'm...sorry,' he said curtly, opening the door to her suite.

Blindly she walked in, emotion robbing her of speech. She heard the door close and she drew a breath, preparing to release her emotions now that he had gone. But then there was a movement behind her and when she whirled around, her eyes huge with unshed tears, she saw that he was still standing there, his shoulders riding high with tension.

'Yes. I understand what you must feel,' she jerked out, knowing so well what his brother's betrayal meant to a man like Dante, whose pride and sense of family honour were of great importance to him.

And she knew, too, how hard it had hit Dante to know that his wife had been raped. Whatever sympathy he felt for her, it would be the ultimate humiliation for such a proud man.

'I don't think you do,' he said through his teeth. 'I can never forgive myself.'

'Yourself?' She frowned, puzzled.

'I am responsible for what has happened,' he said, his face bleak and cold. 'I turned a blind eye to Guido's questionable behaviour. I believed him above others, including you, my wife. If it's any consolation, I am in torment. I will never forgive myself for what he and I have done to you.' His voice was shaking and she wanted to put her arms around him in sympathy but he was untouchable at that moment, horribly distant and contained as if he was preparing for their permanent separation. He drew in a rasping breath, his eyes as dark as coal. 'You must hate the name of Severini.'

'Guido…told you everything that happened?' she ventured.

'Everything,' Dante said, almost inaudibly, his mouth a harsh twist in his stony face.

But he was still ignorant of the cruellest twist of fate, Miranda thought in despair. Dante had yet to learn that his wife was pregnant by his brother! She let out a low moan and Dante stiffened. What must be going through his mind? And when she told him of her condition—as she must…

She felt chills icing her spine, dreading the months she would be carrying a child born of rape. Would she ever feel anything for Guido's child? Could she honestly find it in her heart to love an innocent baby created by such a hideous act?

Thinking of the years she might be struggling to find some scrap of affection for a second, unwanted child, she put her hands to her face and moaned again.

'I don't understand. Why did he hurt Lizzie? Why me?'

Dante's face darkened like thunder and she shuddered, afraid of him. 'Lizzie rejected him. It was the final straw as far as he was concerned. So he thought of a way to pay her back.'

'But to go to such extremes—!'

'His feelings were extreme. Your sister was right,' he bit. 'He's been ferociously jealous of me all my life. He has hated me ever since we were small. What he…did to you wasn't, he said, personal. It was purely to hurt me.'

Not personal! Nothing could be more intrusive or humiliatingly personal! With an effort she bit back the things she wanted to say. What was the point?

'I see.'

Dante winced. Desperately she longed to caress his stone-hard face and ease his pain. But they were irreconcilable because of her pregnancy and so she had to let the barriers come down again and shut him from her life as if he had never existed. Or she'd go mad with grief.

'Guido confessed that he wanted to ruin my marriage. That he fed me the lies about your infidelity—and pretended you were chasing him. He…' Dante's white teeth snagged at his lip and then with an effort he continued. 'As I said, he admitted that he'd spiked *your* drink with the same rape drug. He thought I was still in Italy and that he had plenty of time to…'

'To rape me!' she breathed, speaking the vile words at last.

They hung in the air, polluting it. Neither of them could escape the fallout of that terrible act of malice now or pretend it had never happened. Her eyes closed tightly. She felt sick. To think of those vile hands touching her, that body pressed close to hers…

And she carried his foul seed inside her body. When all the time she'd longed for Dante's child, a brother or sister for Carlo… Oh, God! What was she going to do?

'That was his plan. But he didn't,' Dante rasped on an out-breath. 'You must know that, of course.'

'Know what?' she muttered from her pit of misery.

'That he didn't succeed!' he blurted out hoarsely. 'I interrupted him!'

Her eyes opened so wide that they hurt. *'What did you say?'*

'He didn't do what he'd intended,' Dante grated. 'I am sure of that. I know he's a liar, but he knew that he had to tell me the absolute truth.' His mouth twisted. 'Perhaps that was because I had his neck under my heel at the time. I demanded to know what had happened, good or bad. He says that when he discovered how close I was to the house he panicked, flinging on his clothes just in time. I know he was speaking the truth because he seemed bitter that he hadn't succeeded. You weren't violated by him, Miranda.'

'I—I hadn't realised!' she gasped.

'Think about it. Try to remember how you felt afterwards.'

There was a long pause. She didn't want to cast her mind back, but she did.

'I felt…sick. I was bruised,' she said eventually, her heart bumping hard.

'The nightmare. Recall it. Where did it end?' he asked almost gently.

'I never wanted to go that far into my memory,' she whispered.

'You must. Now. This once. And then forget it.'

Closing her eyes, she went through it all, this time right to the end. And there Guido was, lying on top of her—not totally naked, only his trousers discarded, and although he was pawing her and trying to remove his briefs… She flinched, as if from his touch. And opened her eyes.

The breath slid from her lungs in shuddering relief. 'I remember now. He reached for his mobile—and spoke while he was—' she bit her lip, blushing furiously '—while he was removing his pants. After a while he suddenly rolled away!' she croaked, beginning to shake. 'Oh, dear heaven, I think he is telling the truth. If this is true—'

'It is. I am sure of it.'

It was wonderful news. Why wasn't he taking her in his

arms? Her eyes grew smoky with distress. This should be a moment of joy. Instead, she was realising to her horror that he just didn't want to be married to a woman who'd been stripped naked by his brother and mauled about. The episode had blighted their relationship and, as he'd said, it had cracked their marriage beyond all repair. So she had lost him, after all.

CHAPTER THIRTEEN

HER entire body slumped with defeat. Bleakly she tried to maintain her dignity. In her heart she wanted to rant and rage, but that wouldn't do any good. Dante was set against her and unfortunately emotion wasn't rational. Either you adored someone or you didn't—and his love wasn't strong enough to overcome his revulsion and the trauma of it all.

She steeled her heart. There were practical things to consider now. Getting Lizzie better and helping her to return to England, for instance. Miranda paled. And she must start packing her own things up, saying…goodbye… She felt hot tears scouring her eyes and fiercely blinked them back.

'Miranda,' Dante said in a harsh and pained whisper. 'I feel terrible about this. I owe you and Lizzie my heartfelt apologies.' He turned away, his head bowed. 'My family has dishonoured you,' he muttered. 'Women are to be cherished and protected and you and Lizzie have suffered the most disgusting assault—both attacks being carried out under my roof. I am personally responsible and I can never forget. I will think of it for the rest of my life. I realise how much you must loathe me for bringing you so much heartache and grief. For not believing you, not trusting you. I can only apologise but I know that isn't enough. I can never make things right again. All I can do is to make sure you are well cared for and want for nothing. It's not much. I wish I could turn the clock back. Kill my stupid family pride. Open my eyes to my brother's faults. But it's too late. I know that. Too much has happened and things will never be the same between us. It's over. I realise that. I'm not stupid.'

Amazed, she stared at his tense back. Hope spiralled within her. Perhaps she'd misread the situation. It dawned on her that he was terribly upset and desperately sorry for the distress she'd suffered. Blaming himself and taking the guilt on his own shoulders. Was that why he wasn't holding her close?

'Oh, Dante!' she whispered longingly, and he flinched as if she'd stabbed him in the heart. 'Dante,' she said with all the love she could muster.

'Don't speak kindly to me!' he grated, his fists bunching. 'I don't deserve it! Do you know how badly I feel about my behaviour? How much it's ripping me apart?'

'Yes. I have an idea,' she said softly.

In her bones she felt sure he was aching to take her in his arms. It was a chance she had to take. One last risk of her vulnerable heart. She had nothing to lose but her pride—and what price that, if it won his love?

Quietly she went to face him. Put her hands on his chest. Saw how hard he was clenching his jaw, how resolutely he avoided her gaze. He pulled back, staring at her in alarm.

'Don't touch me. I couldn't bear it,' he muttered. 'Just go. My solicitor—'

'Dante.'

His hands trembled. His mouth quivered at the turned-down corner. Oh, yes. She knew all about self-control. Knew the tell-tale signs that betrayed what lay beneath. The short, shallow breathing. The rigidity of the body.

Her palm slid out to him again and she felt his heart thudding so violently that it seemed it might leap right out of his ribcage.

'Dante,' she murmured again, with deep tenderness and love. And he swallowed. A give-away. Emotion was filling his throat as it was choking hers. She swallowed too. 'It was Guido who tried to dishonour me. And he failed. It's not your fault. You can't be responsible for him—'

'I am,' he said, the words expelled on hot, angry breath. 'That's the trouble. I failed to keep him in check. Didn't pay attention to the signs that he needed guidance…' He bit his lip and forged on grimly. 'He will be punished. I will see to that. And…it will be made public. No one here will ever accept him into their company again. When his sentence has been completed he will have to go abroad, but you can be sure that I'll keep a watch on him. No woman must ever go through what you did. I can't believe I have an animal for a brother!' he groaned.

'He's your blood. But he is his own man,' she insisted. 'But you,' she said, letting her fingers walk up to his pulsing throat. 'What are you intending to do?'

He looked at her with hopeless pain in his eyes as if he contemplated a bleak future. 'I don't know,' he jerked. 'Fling myself into work, I suppose. You can have the house. And Carlo, of course. I'd like some access,' he said with heart-rending difficulty. 'But I won't bother you. I'll find somewhere in Como to live. You—you'll be all right. I promise. You'll have everything you want.'

His heart was breaking, she knew it. And something told her that this was nothing to do with losing his honour, his beloved house, or even total contact with Carlo. It was the way he looked at her as if his eyes were hungrily seeking to record everything about her, to store up memories for the future. The utter desolation of his expression told her more than his strained words.

'I won't have my heart's desire. And nor will you,' she said, her gaze steady on his.

He flinched. 'I don't deserve to have anything I want.'

Now she felt sure. Her eyes kindled, her heart aching. 'But you are as much an innocent victim as I am—'

With a muttered exclamation he pulled away but she caught his arm and hung on. 'Please!' he gritted. 'I let you down. I didn't trust you—'

'Apparently with good reason,' she said soberly.

'If I'd only stopped to think…' His hand raked through his hair. 'Through my own stupidity I've caused you untold misery. Now it's my turn to be in hell, to be punished.'

'That would be a shame when you could be in paradise instead,' she said anxiously, sliding her body against his.

He groaned and held her tightly as if he couldn't help himself. 'Miranda!' he growled. 'Don't torture me like this. You don't know what—'

'Yes, I do,' she said, standing on tiptoe and kissing his angry, tense mouth. When it didn't soften, she looked at him in despair. 'I'm trying to tell you something and you're too deaf and blind to notice!' she cried. 'I love you. You love me. What's the problem?'

'It can't be.' He looked down at her helplessly. 'Not after everything that's happened.'

'Dante. You are a loyal and loving man. All your life you cared for and watched over your brother as I cared for Lizzie. I know how you feel. Every flaw in Guido's character you see as a reflection on you. I felt the same with Lizzie. Her way-wardness was somehow my fault. But the two of them are adults. They are responsible for their own actions. Maybe we have guided and helped, maybe we've made mistakes where they're concerned, indulged them and made allowances or tried to compensate too much...I don't know. But in the end they are masters of their own destiny. You are not your brother's keeper. He has walked his own path and made his own choices. It's not your fault that you were popular—other than the fact that you truly deserved people's affection.' She gazed at him earnestly, impassioned in her need to make him understand that he shouldn't bear his brother's burden of guilt. 'You and he are separate people. You are such a good man. You feel a duty to shoulder his sins because you are a man of great honour and feeling. But you have already been punished enough. I can see that.' Her voice softened. 'It has been hell for you, as it has been for me. But I won't let Guido succeed in his aim. Do you understand?'

'Succeed?' He frowned, uncomprehending.

'He wanted to break us up,' she said simply. 'But we mustn't let that happen because our love is stronger than that, isn't it? You are everything to me. I have no intention of watching you walk away. The nightmare is over, Dante. Let's shut the door on it and walk into the light again. Together.'

There was a long silence while he stared into her pleading

eyes. He swallowed. Licked his lips. Bit them and shook his head as if to clear his brain. 'I—I—' he choked and came to a grinding halt, clearly overcome with emotion.

'Oh, for heaven's sake!' With great tenderness and love, she smiled. 'Pretend I'm a cockroach and kiss me, you idiot!'

His eyes closed. With a helpless groan, he lowered his head and his mouth descended on hers. Warm. Searching. Sweet. She sighed with happiness. Everything would be all right now.

'But—'

'No buts!' she reproved, her hands linking behind his head. And she pulled him closer because they'd almost lost one another and her desperation to bind them together again made her kisses frantic.

'My darling!' he groaned. 'I can't believe this is happening. You truly forgive me?'

'Forgive? I know what was stacked against me. Any red-blooded man would have acted as you did, felt as you did. There's nothing to forgive.'

'Miranda!' he mumbled. 'I can't believe it. This is more than I imagined... In my mind I had made plans...seen a cold and loveless future. Never to see you again, to have contact only through Carlo... I couldn't bear it but I knew that was to be my fate. But every time I thought of what lay ahead for me, my heart was torn to pieces,' he said gently. 'I love you so much and I always have. You are my light, my soul, my reason for existing.'

'How lovely!' she sighed. 'Just how I feel about you,' she whispered.

With a shaky laugh, he kissed her again and it was a very long time before they came up for air.

'I still don't understand how you can forgive me so easily,' he wondered.

'I told you. I don't see you as responsible—and because my love is bigger than any petty resentment,' she said simply. 'I know how hard it's been for you and I have felt your pain and I've wanted to ease it. Your welfare and happiness is important to me because I care about you so very, very much.'

He kissed her long and slow. 'You are amazing, Miranda.. Generous, big-hearted, loving. I am the luckiest man in the world. We'll be happy, us and Carlo. A proper family again.'

He smiled, a radiance lighting his face, and she felt the doubts and burdens of the past slip away.

'We have a wonderful future,' she murmured, kissing him lovingly. Her eyes shone as he smiled down at her with such adoration in his eyes that it made her catch her breath.

'I have a suggestion,' he said, stroking her cheek with his forefinger. His lips tenderly took possession of hers. 'Why don't we have a second wedding, here in Bellagio?'

Delighted, she smiled broadly. 'With ribbons and bows and banners and flags?' she cried eagerly. 'And photographs by the lake and—'

'All that and more. Bells, fireworks, the biggest celebration Bellagio has ever seen,' he said with an affectionate laugh. He looked at her, bemused. '*Mia cara!* I can't believe we're together at last! It was hell thinking you'd been unfaithful. kept wanting to be with you, to see you and hold you—and couldn't understand why. You were worthless, it seemed, and yet I still adored you! I had to fight all my instincts to remain cold and hard—'

'You succeeded!' She gave a wry smile. 'But I know what you mean. I did my best to hate you too but my heart kept telling me otherwise.'

'Perhaps we should rely on what our hearts tell us in future.' He smiled down at her, his hands touching her face in wonder. And he held her in a tight hug, crushing her to him. 'I look ahead and I see such happiness for us,' he said softly. 'The three of us—'

'*Ohhhh!*' she screeched suddenly, making him jump back in great alarm.

'Darling! What is it?' he demanded urgently. 'Are you hurt? What's the matter?'

The future. The *three* of them. How could she have forgot ten?

'Miranda!'

Her eyes closed. She felt herself swaying, the world whirling about. And then she was being picked up, carried lovingly until she was curled up in Dante's lap and he was stroking her forehead, frantically asking her to speak to him.

'Tell me!' he demanded urgently. 'Tell me what it is and I will deal with it. You must have no pain, no misery, no—'

'I've been a fool!' she gulped, her eyes startled and huge. 'I've only just realised…'

'What?' he asked tensely. 'Miranda, you're not saying that we—that we're not to be together after all—'

'No! Relax. It's something wonderful. Lovely,' she purred. 'Something that will make you very, very happy. I promise. A perfect ending to all of this.'

'What? I don't understand!' he complained.

She beamed. Kissed him till he relaxed, groaned and kissed her back hungrily. They snuggled up. She felt the warmth of his arms around her, his loving face nestled against hers.

How could she have forgotten something so important? It had only just dawned on her.

The child she was carrying…must be Dante's.

With a cry of joy, she flung her arms around his neck and hugged him ecstatically. Dante held her closer still.

'You're not making sense,' he husked in her ear.

Laughing, she looked into his dark, inky black eyes and a huge swell of emotion rose within her. This was the man she loved and he would know that, every day of his life. Never again would she hold back. Her feelings would be given full rein because she knew how much he loved her and how much she could trust him with her vulnerable heart. Glowing with an inner radiance, she smiled up at him.

And murmured softly, 'I have such wonderful news for you, my darling. The best news in the world.' Her hand went to her abdomen.

Dante's gaze followed the movement and he stiffened. His hand turned her face to his as it dawned on him what she meant.

'Not… You don't mean…!'

Softly her lips pressed against his warm mouth. 'Yes,' she whispered. 'I'm pregnant. You'll be a father again and Carlo will have a baby brother or sister.'

Dante drew in a long, shuddering breath. She noticed that there were tears of joy in his eyes just before he drew her close with great tenderness.

'A new life,' he said huskily into her small ear. 'My love has come back to me and she carries our child!' His hand splayed over hers as if protecting their baby from all harm. She felt the warmth of his palm and it seemed to her that they were enveloped in a blanket of profound love. He lifted her chin and kissed her long and slow till she felt as if her head was swimming with happiness. 'I love you more than I can say,' he proclaimed. 'My life will be devoted to you, and to our children. You have my entire heart. Every beat of it is for you.'

Miranda felt a tug at her own heart. Sighing, she slid her arms around Dante's neck and gave herself up to his impassioned embrace. They had become one again. And they would be together forever, their bodies, their souls and their lives as one. Their love had been strengthened and nothing, no one would ever come between them.

'Bed,' he said huskily.

'Bed,' she agreed. And unsteadily they went upstairs, checking Carlo, holding hands while they watched him sleep with the sweet innocence that always clutched at Miranda's chest and made her feel so overwhelmed with emotion. Then slowly they went to Dante's room, where he tenderly undressed her, his hands shaking uncontrollably. The sweetness of their love-making obliterated the terrible recent events. It wiped out the past and sealed the future.

They slept like babies, dreamily content and knowing that their whole lives lay ahead of them like a glittering path. And if Carlo was surprised the next morning by their mutual, almost childish exuberance, he was also delighted. His beloved *mama* and *papa* were together again and that was all he cared about. So he indulged them, playing chase and hide-and-seek